WELCOME TO ALL YOUR STORIES MAGAZINE
WE HOPE YOU ENJOY THE SELECTION WE
HAVE CHOSEN FROM SUBMISSIONS SENT BY
WRITERS FROM AROUND THE WORLD.

This magazine is published bi-monthly and if you would like to submit your work check the guidelines on the website.
https://allyourstories.com
Submission email.
submissions@allyourstories.com
Next issue deadline. 18th February2024
Publication date. 1st April 2024

There is a sister magazine All Your Poems more information can be found on the website https://allyourpoems.com

Happy Reading.

Cover Art by SGP The Peace River, Florida USA

Contents

Editor's Choice
Granny Takes a Trip — Jane Risdon
Non-Fiction
Stir Fried — Rekha Valliappan
Why I Bother to Write — Roger Knight
Birthday Memories — Elisha Alladina
Musical Memories of a Bexley Girl — J. A. Newman
A Treasure Lost for Ever — Lavern Spencer McCarthy

Travel
Holy Island — Heather Haigh
The Ratman of Edinburgh — Hannah McIntyre
The Place Less Visited — Julie Watson
The Fifteen Minute Tourist Escape — Meredith Stephens
Quick Reads
That's His Boy — Con Chapman
Memory — Barbara Hull
A Flower by Any Other Name — Michael Shawyer
Meandering Intermittent Revolutions — Linda Hibbin
Three Flash Fiction Stories — Christopher T. Dabrowski

1912 — DC Diamondopolous
Divorced — Andrew Senior
Memoir
Dance Republic — Chiara Vascotto
Fiction Short Stories
Journey Across Dartmoor — Andy Stewart
The Old Ladies Bench — Jean Ende
On the Beach — S. Berenstein

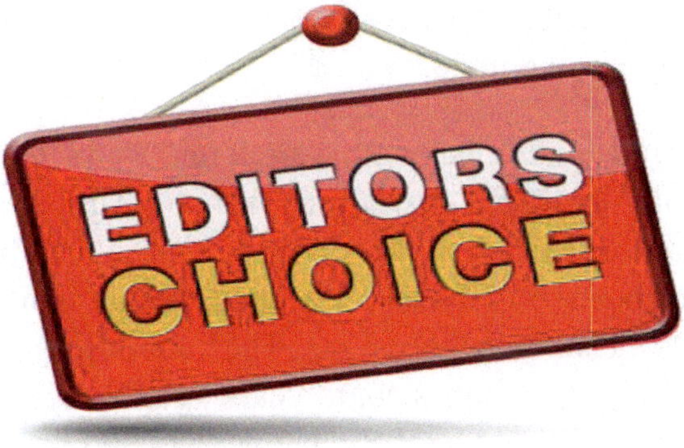
EDITORS
CHOICE

Granny Takes a Trip (Fiction)
by Jane Risdon

Opening her own book shop had always felt like a pipe dream for Tabitha. Something she'd imagined doing but never really believed would happen. But happen it had. She could hardly believe her good fortune. Pinching herself for reassurance, she looked around her own piece of heaven, sighing with delight as the summer sunshine crept across the oak floorboards towards the shelves of books with all their glorious covers and hidden delights. As she awaited her first customers panic gripped her throat. Of course, there would be customers she reassured herself not for the first time. There had to be.

Tabitha didn't have to wait long. News of the new book shop opening had been the talk of the tiny rural Berkshire village she'd moved to earlier in the summer. Once, a mobile library had served the locals but if they'd wanted to buy a book, a trip into Ascot or Windsor was necessary. The mobile library had stopped servicing the local villages some years ago. Now, at last, there was somewhere locals could call their own. As soon as Tabitha placed the 'open' sign in the bay window of her tiny store, two excited elderly ladies stepped across the threshold. Her first potential customers.

'Good morning ladies, welcome to Granny Takes a Trip.' Tabitha offered her hand to the taller of the two women, a broad smile on her face.

'Well, hello and welcome to Upper Pond Place, I'm Alice Deeping, I live near what was once the Post Office,' the handsome, elegant woman said. Tabitha shook her hand and smiled.

'Yes, and I'm Sapphire Deeping and I live next door to Alice in what was once the bakery. We're sisters,' the slightly smaller woman said. She stretched her hand towards Tabitha who shook it, noticing her firm handshake. She was dressed as elegantly as her sister and smiled just as broadly. 'We are so excited to have a book shop back in the village.'

Cont.

'I'm Tabitha, it's lovely to meet you both.' She hadn't had time to meet anyone from the village since she inherited her new home, and business premises, and was delighted to find her first locals so friendly. 'I'd no idea there used to be a book shop in the village,' she said.

'Oh yes, for many years, and then one day the owner just upped and disappeared, without so much as a goodbye or explanation.' Sapphire sounded excited.

'That's right. Abigail was the owner back then. Let's see, it's got to be thirty years ago now,' Alice said, her eyes suddenly bright. 'Opened her shop one morning, went inside, and was never seen again.' Both sisters shook their heads, raised their eyebrows, and sighed, almost in perfect time.

'Goodness me,' Tabitha was intrigued. 'That is odd. Seriously, no-one ever heard from her again?'

'No. The postman delivered a letter for her as she opened up that morning and she took it, went back into the shop, and vanished.' Sapphire was almost bouncing on the balls of her feet with excitement. 'She left without taking a thing with her, so they say.'

'That's interesting,' Tabitha pursed her lips. 'There's a load of stuff in boxes in the attic but I've not had time to go through them yet, I really must take a look, but there weren't any books here when I took over.'

'Oh do, we'd love to know if there are any clues, wouldn't we, Alice?' Sapphire's cheeks were pink, matching her silk scarf.

'Sappy darling, you're so nosey, perhaps Tabitha prefers to keep things private and to herself.' Her sister nudged her arm. Secretly just as intrigued.

Cont.

'Let me look first.' Tabitha was tempted to shut the shop and go rummage in the attic right away. 'What do you know about my grandmother? I never met her. She gifted me this building, some money, and shares, along with all the contents over 30 years ago, but I was not to benefit until I turned forty, which I did last March.' She took a deep breath, 'no-one mentioned this had been a book shop before, but I was told the premises had to retain the name 'Granny Takes a Trip,' hence the name hasn't changed.'

Both women gasped. 'You're Abigail's granddaughter?'

'Yes, I am, but I've no idea what happened to her; no-one has. She left instructions with her solicitor, I guess around the time she disappeared, and I've just been informed, following my birthday.' Tabitha hadn't thought anything of the bequest. Alone in the world, she'd never met, or heard anything of her grandmother or her wishes until the letter arrived arranging an appointment with a London solicitor.

'She must be dead; I wonder what happened to her after she disappeared?' Alice couldn't contain herself, 'it's all so exciting.'

'I don't know if she's dead or not, or anything about her life,' Tabitha said thoughtfully. 'Now I'm intrigued about her. It is a delicious mystery.'

'It is indeed. How exciting. We love mysteries, don't we Alice?' Sapphire grabbed her sister's elbow, her eyes wide and shining. 'But she must be dead, she was about your age when she vanished, or even older, I've no idea.'

The shop door opened, and two girls entered. They didn't look up from their smart phones as Tabitha said good morning to them. 'Hi,' they replied in unison and wandered to the back of the shop. Tabitha watched them browse a few shelves before sitting crossed legged on the floor, phones still active.

Cont.

'Excuse me ladies,' she left the sisters and walked up to the girls. 'Can I help you at all?'

'Nah, we're fine thanks. It's getting hot outside and we thought we'd take a look at the shop.' One of them looked up briefly. Her friend didn't bother.

'Are you looking for anything in particular? Do you wish to use the internet?'

'Nah, like she said, we're hot so we're cooling off in here.' The other girl spoke without her thumbs stopping scrolling through her phone.

'Sorry to disappoint you ladies, but this is not somewhere to cool off, this is a busy shop, and I cannot allow you to clutter the place.' Tabitha was outraged at their cheek. 'Please buy a book or leave.'

Both girls looked up at her, shock, and disbelief on their over made-up faces. 'You serious or what?' One asked, glancing at the other.

'Jenny Goodyear, you get yourself and Mandy Flintock outside now.' Alice had come up beside Tabitha and waved her hand at the girls. 'I'll be seeing your mothers' at the W.I. this evening. Do you want me to tell them how rude you've been?'

Both girls rose reluctantly and shuffled towards the door. 'Nothing special in here anyway,' one of them shouted over her shoulder as she slammed the door hard.

Cont.

'They're not bad girls as a rule, just bored. School holidays you know.' Sapphire sighed, 'nothing for them to do around here. The village is dying, all the youngsters are moving away. We've a few original families here, but mostly we have second homeowners, weekends only.'

The door opened and an elderly gentleman with a stick entered. 'Morning ladies,' he nodded to the sisters. 'You must be the newcomer.' He stared at Tabitha. 'Wonder how long you'll last?'

'Gordon Knight, you really take the biscuit. What a welcome for Tabitha. You should be ashamed of yourself considering she's Abigail's granddaughter.' Alice scolded the old man who took a pair of spectacles from his jacket breast pocket and peered at Tabitha as if she were a specimen in a museum display.

'Get away with you, Abigail? Who says?'

'I say, Mr Knight. I'm her granddaughter although I've never met her.' Tabitha went behind her counter, feeling very unsettled at the strange people venturing into her shop since it opened. 'However, it seems to me you all knew her.'

'Don't let him rile you dear.' Sapphire scowled at the man. 'He's a right pain in the aspidistra most of the time. He's not happy unless he's moaning.'

'I'll have a look around, see if you've got anything worthwhile. You carry on gossiping. Don't mind me.' He wandered deeper into the shop leaving the two women shaking their heads.

Tabitha had to laugh, 'anymore where he came from?'

'Mostly older folk living here these days, and those who still have their marbles will remember your grandmother. She was popular and many of the local men had their eye on her, Gordon included.'

Cont.

'Did you know your grandfather?' Alice asked, ignoring the piercing look Sapphire was giving her.

'No. I imagine he died before I was born but I can't be sure. My mother and father died when I was ten and a distant cousin of my mother's looked after me until I went to boarding school. She never knew anything about the family, well, anything she wanted to share – and as I was away most of the time I never got to talk to her about much. When I left school and went to university she got married and went to South Africa. I haven't had much contact with her since then. Apparently she's got Alzheimer's now.'

'You poor girl,' said Sapphire, her hand over her heart. 'That's so sad.'

'You don't miss what you never had, I guess.' Tabitha smiled. 'I'm fine thanks. I loved school and university, and my life has been full, so far,' she laughed.

'I'll take this,' the old man banged a book on the counter. 'You still here?' He glared at the sisters.

'My first sale, Mr Knight, thanks so very much.' Tabitha placed the Graham Greene novel in a paper bag and the old man swiped his card on the payment machine. He took the receipt and muttered, 'bloody daylight robbery if you ask me.'

'Thanks so much, I appreciate your custom.' Tabitha held the door for him.

'Only came to take a look at you,' he muttered as he left.

The sisters burst out laughing. 'Expensive being nosey,' giggled Alice.

The door opened and a tall man in dark cords and a black leather jacket entered, he smiled at the ladies and nodded to Tabitha. 'Thought I'd have a browse if that's all right?'

Cont.

'Feel free, welcome,' Tabitha smiled and noted Alice and Sapphire nudging each other.

The man headed to the back of the store as the ladies raised their eyebrows and Alice whispered, 'another stranger, how exciting.'

'Good looking too,' Sapphire added. 'Look, we'd best be off, we can't stand nattering all morning and you have a business to run. We'll be back in a few days to see how you are. We just wanted to welcome you to the village.' She grabbed Alice by the arm and almost frog-marched her out the door.

'Bye ladies, and thanks,' Tabitha said to their departing backs.

Before she could move, the door opened again, and the postman entered. He handed her a bundle of letters and circulars held together with a rubber band. 'You be the new owner,' he nodded. 'I'm Ted. You want to know anything about the village or where everything is and what happens here, you ask that Sapphire and Alice. Oracles they are. What they don't know ain't worth forgetting.' He nodded and left the shop.

Tabitha giggled and sorted through her mail. Sensing the man in black was watching her from across the counter, she glanced up, smiling.

'I'll take this please,' he said, handing her a copy of the latest John Le Carrè novel. 'I enjoy spy novels. Mysteries intrigue me.' Hestared hard at her, making her feel uncomfortable, wishing the ladies had stayed a little longer. Handing her cash, he held his hand out for the receipt. 'Don't bother with a bag; got to save the planet and all that.'

Cont.

'Very commendable of you.' Was all Tabitha could think to say. 'Thank you.'

'No, thank you – Tabitha,' he said, as he shut the door behind him. Tabitha's chin almost hit her chest. How the hell did he know her name? The cheek of him, she thought. She shrugged, he must've heard the sisters call her that, she decided. Yet she shivered, unsettled, as if he'd just walked over her grave.

###

The store was busy the rest of the day, and by the time she put the closed sign up she'd sold more books than she'd expected and had met several of the village locals. Most were indeed elderly, and many recalled her grandmother. Word got around quickly.

It was still warm out, and after having a bite to eat she decided to walk along the river to the pub. It had a lovely beer garden where she took her glass of the local cider, feeling somewhat uncomfortable with the scrutiny of – the mostly male – drinkers inside when she ordered her drink. Sunlight glinted on the water as she watched various ducks and swans gliding in and out of the vegetation. Tabitha breathed deeply, enjoying the fragrance of the hedges of Rosa Rugose lining the garden path nearby. Few drinkers had ventured outside, and she began to relax as the sinking sun warmed her face whilst she sipped her drink.

She became aware of someone standing behind her. Goose bumps spread along her arms as she turned, shielding her eyes with her hand as she strained to see who it was behind her. The man in black stared at her for a few moments and then walked into the pub. Tabitha felt shaken by him and his silence. Who was he? What was he thinking, standing behind her like that, scaring the daylights out of her for no apparent reason? She wanted to follow him and ask, but she was rooted to the spot. After a few minutes she rose, drained her glass, and gingerly entered the pub. She scanned the small bar area and the adjoining dining room, but he wasn't there.

Cont.

'Excuse me.' Approaching the barman, she asked, 'did you see a man dressed all in black come in just now?'

'Nope,' he mumbled, polishing a glass.

'He's quite good-looking. He was wearing a black leather jacket and black cords.'

'Fancy your chances do you?' Gordon Knight came up and stood beside her, nodding knowingly at the barman who laughed and went to tend to an elderly customer.

'Mr Knight, certainly not. It's just he was in the shop earlier and a moment ago he stood behind me in the garden, without uttering a word,' she hurriedly explained. 'I wondered if he wanted to talk to me, that's all.'

'Don't know him. Saw him in your shop but he's not from around here.'

'He's quite unsettling.'

'Ah, is that what they call it these days?' Mr Knight laughed. 'In my day they called it chemistry.'

###

Tabitha's first week passed quickly without further incident, and she settled into her daily routine with pleasure. The two sisters called in with an invitation to church on Sunday which she declined. They wanted to know if she'd explored her attic and were anxious to hear if she'd found anything. She said she hadn't looked yet. She'd actually completely forgotten about the attic, only the man in black – as she thought of him – occupied her thoughts in quieter moments. He intrigued her. He'd not reappeared since he was in the pub garden, and she'd gone back twice to see if he might return. He hadn't.

Cont.

Sunday morning, Tabitha climbed the ladder to the attic containing her grandmother's possessions with more than a little excitement, if not apprehension. She hoped she'd find something about her family and especially Abigail, in amongst the dust-covered boxes and suitcases.

The first few boxes contained the usual stuff one puts away 'in-case' it's ever needed again: old lamps, broken vases which never got fixed and lots of books. She worked throughout the morning without finding anything of any real interest. Taking a break for lunch, she was back in the attic within an hour. This time she started work on the suitcases. Most of them contained an assortment of clothes, probably put away for the season. As she worked through them realisation dawned; the clothes weren't for any particular season. There was a variety of items wearable all year round, including coats, shoes, and handbags. Strange.

Tabitha looked more closely at each case and it's contents. It occurred to her that they appeared to have been packed hurriedly; nothing folded neatly and put away with care. Why would her grandmother just throw clothes into suitcases? She sat back on her heels and really scrutinised everything. The clothes were of good quality and fashionable for the period Abigail would've worn them. Tabitha wondered what her grandmother might have taken with her when she disappeared from her store and village life. Had she taken anything?

Did anyone think Abigail's disappearance strange, sudden, perhaps not a little sinister? Why did they all assume she'd just gone off with someone, leaving of her own accord? She felt unsettled about her vanishing without a trace. No-one seemed to be concerned at all. Had the police been informed? From what she'd discovered about her grandmother — pretty-well nothing, she realised — she'd got the impression she was something of a looker, a popular woman, a little secretive.

Cont.

Whatever happened to her? Did she 'go off' with a man, as everyone inferred, but if so who? No-one she'd spoken with, ever mentioned knowing who her grandmother's supposed lover might have been. Tabitha chatted to several customers over the last week, who'd visited mostly out of curiosity, she was sure; a few even purchased books. They knew her grandmother, but they all said she kept herself to herself away from the store. So why assume a man was involved? Perhaps it was typical of the times; a man must be at the route of everything where women were concerned.

Tabitha turned to the last suitcase, but again there wasn't anything to give her a clue as to why her grandmother had left behind what she was convinced constituted her whole wardrobe. Was it possible someone else had packed her things away? Why?

The rest of the attic held nothing of interest. Frustrated at the lack of clues, Tabitha started towards the ladder. She turned ready to make her descent onto the landing. Putting a foot on the first rung, she noticed a shelf tucked into the eaves almost hidden in the gloom on her left side. A large standard lamp was in front, and she almost ignored it except that something beyond, glinted. Moving back into the attic she pulled the lamp aside, and stared at the shelf upon which she found an old copper kettle. Nothing else was visible first glance. Moving the kettle aside for a closer look she heard a metallic rattle. Removing the lid, she tipped the kettle upside down. A brass key fell out with a white envelope. Her heart skipped a beat as she examined the envelope with shaking fingers. Taking a deep breath, she ripped it open.

The handwritten note was signed Abigail Mont Morris, Tabitha noticed, upon turning to the last of several pages. Her heart thudded, seeing her grandmother's handwriting - such a thrill. She returned to the first page and read. When she'd finished she shook her head in disbelief. The former owner of Granny Takes a Trip left a safety deposit box key, to be used in the event of her death or disappearance, when all would be explained by the contents.

Cont.

Tabitha hurried down the ladder. She raced to her garage for her car, before realising it was Sunday. It was going to be a long wait until the bank opened on Monday morning.

After a sleepless night, Monday morning arrived sunny, warm, and full of promise. After a hasty breakfast, Tabitha drove into Oxford and found a parking space not too far from her grandmother's bank. Her heart thudded so loudly she imagined everyone could hear it. She hadn't any idea what she'd find. The letter explained that Abigail's bookshop was the *front* for an *organisation,* and more information would be held in the safety deposit box. Her mind worked over-time, had her grandmother been a drug-runner - the name of the shop might be a clue, she reasoned – or was she a money launderer for gangsters? She hoped and prayed her grandmother was not a criminal, but it didn't bode well so far.

Doing as instructed in the letter addressed to the *finder, or whomever it concerned,* Tabitha asked to see her deposit box and gave the details she'd been given, to the bank clerk, which included a password and a phrase identifying the bearer as the rightful owner. She was taken into a private room and given a long metal box, then left alone.

Shaking, Tabitha used the little key to open her grandmother's box of secrets. Warily, she sat at the table preparing to go through the contents carefully, her heart heavy with worry at what she was about to discover.

###

Cont.

Thirty minutes later, a stunned Tabitha sat in Brown's Tea Rooms and thoughtfully sipped her tea. Well, I never, she mused. Her grandmother planned on someone finding the kettle and its contents one day and hoped they'd access the deposit box— to do what?

'May I join you?' A shadow crossed her table, and she looked up to see the man in black.

'What?'

'May I join you, Tabitha?' He repeated, smiling broadly.

'Why? Just who are you?' she snapped. 'How do you know my name?'

'If I could sit down, I'd tell you.' He pulled up a chair and sat anyway, making her want to smack him. The nerve!

Before she could say another word a waitress produced coffee and a plate of brownies. 'I'm starving,' he said, and offered her the plate. She almost took one but stopped herself in time. She shook her head.

'I asked who you are? What you want with me?' Her voice sounded strangled she knew. She was fuming mad and barely concealing it. 'How do you know me?'

'Tabitha, I know all about you,' he said, before biting into a brownie. 'Let's relax and eat and we can talk after,' he suggested.

Furious at his nerve, Tabitha stood to leave. 'Bugger off and leave me alone,' she hissed as she grabbed her bag.

'Don't be like that, we have so much to chat about and I'm sure you'd like some answers about Abigail and her little box of tricks.' His lips smiled but his eyes did not. 'Sit down.'

###

Cont.

'I don't believe you,' Tabitha was stunned by what the man in black told her. 'She wouldn't, she just wouldn't.'

'And you know this how?' The man almost laughed at the book seller's naivety. 'You never met her, knew nothing of her until you got your little windfall.'

Tabitha didn't have a reply. He was right. She knew next to nothing about her grandmother apart from her disappearance and the contents of the safety deposit. She felt stupid under his amused gaze.

'Sorry love, but it's all true. Grandma Abigail was a Soviet spy. You might not like it and neither, quite frankly, does HM's Secret Intelligence Service, as you can imagine.'

'You're MI5 or whatever?' Tabitha whispered, her eyes scanning the tea rooms suspiciously.

'No names, but yes; I'm *whatever*.' He leaned back in his chair, regarding her carefully. 'You saw the box of tricks, so you know it's true.'

'How do you know about the box?'

'We found the kettle years ago, and the letter. Before my time you understand, but the powers-that-be, decided to leave it all in situ. They expected her contacts to turn up looking for it at some point, but they didn't. No-one was interested until you.'

Tabitha was bewildered. Before she could ask how, he said, 'the whole place is bugged, and every now and again someone listens to the recordings. You set off an alarm when you moved in. Everyone went into melt down wondering just who you really were.' He sighed. 'We searched the whole place and found the box when she first disappeared. Everything was replaced after we'd checked it out, and the waiting began.'

Cont.

'That's mental. If you know everything, why didn't you go after her?' Tabitha leaned forward and said, 'where is she? What happened to her?'

The man in black – he still hadn't introduced himself and Tabitha let it go, thinking he'd probably give a false name anyway – leaned forward and said, quietly, 'I lied. We did remove some items, but you don't need to know about them. Your grandmother was quite a militant in her youth and was on many 'watch lists.' He drained his cup before adding, 'the powers- that-be, back then, decided to watch and wait. It paid off, she operated a 'dead letter drop' at the bookshop. You know what that is?'

'I've seen spy thrillers.' Tabitha stared hard at him. 'You think she was a spy, for the Soviets, yet you let her carry on, why?'

'She was useful, and we fed her contacts and all sorts of nonsense which she passed on to her handlers. It suited us at the time.'

'This is all fascinating and exciting, but you still haven't said what happened to her. I want to know, now.'

'Ah, yes, of course. It seems that on the day she disappeared she received a letter. It was a trigger for her to act; her contacts felt things were hotting up. Thinking she was about to be discovered she cleared out pronto - left everything behind. They lifted her later, we understand. She'd previously decided to leave the key and instructions – in the kettle — with some important papers for her contacts to collect. We got to it first. We waited for someone to come, but no-one did. They got wind the shop was under surveillance, apparently. The place has remained deserted all this time, too hot to touch, and then you turned up. She sent you. Your grandmother was alive and well in Moscow until she died recently, and the rest you know.'

Cont.

'Dead? But why did she leave it all to me?' Tabitha tried to process the information; it was all too much. 'She must've been sure someone would come for the key and documents immediately, and if not, the kettle and its contents leading to the safety deposit box would've been found later. Anyone could've discovered it. It was risky. She couldn't have known I'd find it all these years later.'

'She lived on the edge, craved excitement, her oldest friends said. But, they had no idea about her activities. She was approached at Cambridge University to spy for the Soviets; she enjoyed it. She wasn't really a committed Communist, she was an activist at heart; it was a game which got too serious.' The man watched Tabitha. 'She left some dynamite stuff for the Soviets; we got it first and the contents of her deposit box were replaced with credible but harmless items, which you found. It must've been a shock for you, finding the evidence we left. But she obviously wanted you to have the shop, so it was likely you'd discover her secret.'

'I'm gobsmacked. Seriously. My gran was a spy. It all happened here. Did she do real damage?'

'Oh, yes. Sadly. People died. She was lucky to escape with her life. If we hadn't needed to 'play' her she'd have been taken out a long time ago.'

'There's so much to process, I'm in shock. What happens now?' Tabitha suddenly felt uneasy. 'Are you going to 'take me out,' now I know?'

'You will sign the Official Secrets Act with a written declaration confirming your silence under threat of prosecution, otherwise you're free to continue with your life.'

Cont.

'Do you know why she called the bookshop, 'Granny Takes a Trip?' I can't help thinking it means something.'

'Your grandma was a bit of a hippie in her youth, did the drugs thing, and she'd wanted to give it a name which stuck. Also, it was a message for her contacts later on – out in the open for all to see. She had a sense of humour.'

'Yes, I can see that. I won't change the name, but can I be sure no-one else will mistake me for a spy if I leave it as it is?'

'Not a problem, her contacts are long gone.' The man in black rose. 'I'll be in touch, meantime keep a lid on this,' he leaned over her, menacingly, she thought.

'I won't, I promise,' she said and meant it.

'Good, we don't want to have to rename the shop, 'Granddaughter Takes a Trip.' He winked at her.

'No of course not,' Tabitha said with real conviction.

'You have to laugh at your grandmother, Tabitha, she'd had quite a giggle naming her shop, and a little clairvoyance too, it seems.'

'Clairvoyance?' She was momentarily confused, then laughed, 'Oh yes, 'Granny Takes a Trip,' and she did.'

'Any further questions you might have, can be answered at our next meeting.' He waved as he walked away. 'Be seeing you.'

Tabitha sat for ages after he'd gone, mulling over all she'd discovered about Abigail. She forgot to ask about her life in Russia, how and when she died, and where she's buried. She'd like to visit her grave, if possible now that Russia was more open. Perhaps she'd find out more about the trip her granny had taken all those years ago. Tabitha always wanted family, but cripes, this was something else. More than she'd ever imagined.

Cont.

Her granny was a Soviet spy. Unreal. Another meeting he said. When? How? Why? What a pity she couldn't tell the Miss Deepings.

Tabitha smiled a secret smile as she thought about her grandmother and her shop. Granny Takes a Trip – she certainly did.

nonfiction
(noun)

the branch of literature comprising works of narrative prose dealing with or offering opinions or conjectures upon facts and reality, including biography, history, and the essay.

Stir Fried
By
Rekha Valliappan

'The only real stumbling block is fear of failure. In cooking you've got to have a what-the-hell attitude.' –Julia Child

This or that this or that this or that. A targeted result, whether article or adjective, pronoun or adverb, gourmet or experimentation. Looking down the line is all a matter of objectivity. Expecting your spark of inorganic or homegrown writing to last barely a lesson, to not extend beyond a year, at most, won't work. My efforts to chop and mince may be clumsy, but over time they have built up all around me. I can smell the raw ingredients, the drifts, old paper in stacks, sheets on sheets of decaying compost gathering in old drafts, scribbles that still exist. Chewing on my own writing gets livelier.

However I see many a hopeful writer on many a writing platform express such attitudes. Just into a year of complaints or shorter, outpourings stack up, some are willing to step back, surrender, take leave of their olfactory apparatus with or without that prominent hippocampus at work, assess their victories or failures, as the crisis case may be. And take a break! From writing? *What does that mean!* Cooking does not permit the bottom of the apple barrel to vinegarize. To recalibrate the breaks . . . if two stalks of coriander called for a better recipe would one substitute those with asparagus?

A key part of a storied institution is a functioning odor receptor climbing up for success, blooming for success, living the success, writing for success, smelling the success, cooking for success, possibly cascading in success, where we are hungry for excess of 'suxxess'. A good spice will tear up most dry eyes. I never cook a dish unless it's wildly turmeric-ed. How do we attain such abiding altitudes? By the sensitive application of the olfactory organ. In moderation writing is a subjective endeavor. One takes necessary measures. One hangs onto grab bars, the spatula. One pushes the pinnacle of the stimuli. Lots of things can happen, discordant, improved or resigned. Handling the esophagus invites theoretic existence. The significant obligation for writing belongs

Cont.

to that measured other in us, among us, the plodders, the ramblers, the day-dreamers, the bleeders, the climbers, who, trapped in our outer hard shells, mount the ladders of imagination, to emanate and enchant, to tinker and liquefy, in other words the turtles of industry, not the instant ready mades or mountebanks, in the end.

Without tearing up draft after draft, without head banging on the brick wall over and over, without tap-tapping our closed circuit cranial corridors to stare into Carl Sagan's outer spaces so to speak for a better look at the Milky Way, without bonding into Lady Macbeth's entire monologues of 'blood-smelt' verbiage to connect, without turning our novels or short stories or WIPs into some impossible nature walking project for the future of veganism in a sense, or a compressed chili-faceted pad thai, I have seen smell happen. I am willing to cede my scribbling pen, ink blotter, notepad and all, anchovies, jasmine rice and pomegranate crushed, to the brilliant but cautious daughters of Apollo, the stony but like-minded dashing sons of Medusa out there, even those who claim their olfactory organs are uncomfortably atrophied, acknowledging that they wrangle and make or break at no lesser standards.

To them I say heat up your wok. Throw in your well cubed lines one by one. Old school grid, the colorful cuts go last. They will adjust to the flame. Innovatively yet efficiently, add the seasoning. Sprinkle choice adjectives for greater spice, some adverbs you can trust. The paragraphs absorb the flavors. Place them in last. The purpose of the mixture is the symphony of fragrance it will arouse up your olfactory senses into your inner head. Stir fry the entire lot one last time, thick with sauce, consistent with the desired aromas, then serve, straight from the wok, while crunchy and piping hot.

The longer you stare at the simmering frying pan, floating in flavorful juices, figuring out why it looks as it does, all colorful and toasty, smells as it looks, heady and delicious, concentrating on such trivialities as this or that, lid or no lid, less gravy or more, garnish or stock, lemon or tamarind, rock salt or sea salt, red pepper or corn,

Cont.

minor stuff, but necessary all the same to inflate the rising vapors, to maintain the Machiavellian relish. Throw in more raisins to heighten the smelly ooze, reaching for the ketchup to ultimately level the stir fried conjugations. There is no magical option. Always keep one thick volume of odorous good poetry handy, like a within easy reach drawn and diced cheese platter, as your ultimate nutrition guide, the smellier the better. At the end of the day for your victory lap holding the dish in close contiguity to the range of your nose, the more likely you are going to revise, re-revise, re-re-revise, skewered quartered bits and all. Typical writing standards to the practical and the uninspired! To make the prediction honestly, the old approach is the fresh approach, you are substantially going to imbibe the entire thing, so that scouring the wok within its original scope from recipe to denouement, from conception to conclusion, it no longer resembles anything you had written, errr cooked, before, if at all.

If cross-genre braised integration is not your style or preference for your inflamed nostrils then make the tentative deal. Stay with what works for you in terms of plot and character and setting and floral notes and fruitier texture. Above all stay with the winning writing smells because the love for good writing is a zesty perfume that only you can power up. You will know it when you see it, as in sniff it. It comes in many different varieties over and beyond what your regimented schedule of reading permits. And if you are one of those scent endowed cranks who savor the smell of books, the sweat of decomposing paper in the binding, then so be it, better still, on the record. Because, like me, you may be one specially endowed to delight in the earthy, the moldy, the spicy odor of irresistible vanilla in the book scents to reach writing anesthesia, backdrop, memory and coconut milk commandeered distance.

It is a matter of development. I call it testing the asafetida, since it works. I am no stir fry junkie, nor a wok-guru, like my mom, in fact given my kitchen capabilities I consider myself a peppercorn—hot and delicate, but even I have to admit to book

Cont.

sniffing secrets for those remote scents of petrichor of my childhood to overcome the true meaning in cycles of dejection I have encountered and received over the years from all manner of picky publications. This is a writer's narrative. If there is ever an issue stay true to yourself. Believe in your work. Break the self-worth bubble .

And the dream dies there. You destroy the cookbook. To do a pivot, depending on your life sentences meted out to you, whether in regular standard format, or informally, whether inconsiderately, or kindly, will be the litmus test of the picky publisher. *Not you!* Because, for a writer however emerging, or emerged, new or old, to connect with a publication however seasoned, or developing, current or established, is emotional. What quinoa or coucous does to biriyani rice. On a diplomatic scale of the hundreds of writers who typically submit in an open reading period you don't want to see a same writer being given multiple repeat opportunities within the same publications. It leans towards taste—man-made or acquired. I compare them to charcoal, the kind that burns the best steaks in a cast iron skillet, well seared or not.

Some determined picky picks will go with the adage if a rose smells better than a broccoli it's got to taste better. Well, does it? Unanswered, on the high road the approaches through the measure of the taste buds grow stunted. Creativity gets lost. Still, one does not grab the paprika, douse the dish in excessive soy sauce or throw out the out the wok, building reputations out of all one's failures to persist, even with leftovers. Never let it get to you. I run to my salve, my book shelves of seasoned old smells, their pages browned with ancientness, the older the better.

The thing about sensory perception is your other senses dim. An earthy odor twitches your nose. You take a succession of swift whiffs the more you smell the rot, letting the breeze rifle through the paper pages in rapid succession. Your breath dampens. You hold it

Cont.

in numbed by the essences released, as though the pages in the book are releasing a fresh new long forgotten sweat. For me it is of childhood, memories of my mother stirring a pot over a hot stove in our little kitchen, the flavors of home style cooking, an old chest in which she stored our best tableware for special occasions, my school library where I used to spend my happiest hours. It is a good thing. A mixed bag. In the aloneness of the moment the stimuli runs deep, all the way to the limbic brain stem. You want to hold your breath in, but then you exhale one last time. Your pulse calms in your ears. The oriole enters the dawn with age every day, each day. Reality is able to turn on. Drink up the latest rejection like a new glass of oaked wine, because however much on left field you find yourself, there's always a new pair of discerning eyes who will not pass you by or pass up on your writing that excites them.

    Ultimately, as they say, what tomorrow will look like, everything that a writer writes could just as easily have been written, and was written, by someone else, but not by you. If you are the wildest optimistically wisest cat alive, forgive my analogy, and in this creative business you have got to be the eager one, the samurai with the gleaming chopsticks, because those are the dynamics and sensibilities of good writing, smelling a little of damp rot, the private joy of deep-fried tofu, never mind the smoky onions scent, the unexpected noodles squeeze, you will outrun that last release in the end.

Why I bother to write
by
Roger Knight

You don't write because you want to say something, you write because you've got something to say.

F. Scott Fitzgerald.

Ironically, having reluctantly arrived at that autumnal season of life, I am probably writing more now, compared to when I was a university student or pursuing my former career.

This does beg the question as to why ?. Certainly I have more time on my hands now, but I think the motives are more varied and complex than that.

George Orwell thought that there were four great motives for writing, particularly prose which exists in different degrees in every writer. These were : Sheer egoism, Aesthetic enthusiasm, Historical impulse and Political purpose.

Some of these I can relate to and agree with, I certainly don't agree with the desire to seem clever or to be talked about, but perhaps in a rather vain way, to be remembered after death.

The desire to write something possibly perennial, when all about me is ephemeral, can be compelling.

What I have found though, since leaving life's procession, has been the rapid decline in propinquity and peak experiences I once had, the very material that creates memories and ultimately stories. As a result, I have become stuck in those valleys of reflection, recalling experiences sometimes in granular detail, hence the prose that follows.

Once the ability to make more recent memories tapers off, replaced by monotonous inertia, I simply draw on those past experiences that provide the trigger and material with which to

Cont.

write about.

As a result, I can quote from Anais Nin, taste life twice : in the moment and in retrospect, and it is the retrospect that I relive my life, with more insight, more meaning and a greater appreciation of a particular experience or event, which might be reflected through possible embellishment and hyperbole that most writers are prone to.

This elevates the experience significantly, that may not have been as apparent during the actual moment when it occurred.

It is perhaps because of this, that there is a desire to share my writing with others. Why ? . Because it might have some didactic quality, or simply have an enhancing, even astonishing effect to a possible reader, certainly not to seem clever, as Orwell suggests, or to show off in any way.

There is of course, the psychological motives for writing, such as the slowing of cognitive decline, a replacement raison d'etre, even catharsis and closure.

There is, too, the intrinsic satisfaction of expressing an idea or belief in a cogent insightful way that increases the knowledge and appreciation of it, just as this piece of writing might.

But what really matters to me in the end, is that the story of my life has been mostly written now. Whether or not it has been written well, or worth reading at all, is not so much the point, as record of a life lived ,that I like to think was of some substance, which the remnants of my writing might reveal, to those who might have the inclination and interest to read them.

Birthday Memories
by
Elisha Alladina

"Children waiting for the day they feel good, happy birthday, happy birthday" -Tears For Fears

That time of year, when the focus was on me and my birthday. Mom always planned elaborate parties and I got lots of presents from family and friends, perfectly wrapped with fancy ribbons, like the bows in my hair. Each time I'd get a brand-new stylish dress to wear for the party, and my baby sister would get a mini version of it. Every year, we prepared loot bags of small toys and treats, labelling each one with a friend's name, and wrapped game prizes for them. For my 9th birthday, I got a piano shaped cake, and on my 11th birthday, a musical jewelry box cake, otherwise they were plain store bought ones. When younger in the 80s, I had cabbage patch kids, strawberry shortcake, and doll cakes, all time stamps of my age. We still have pictures of all these creations.

At 40, the only presents I have left are music related ones from my teen years. I got a boom box for my 12th birthday, and I got CD's like Michael Jackson's HIStory and Blood On the Dancefloor, and The Fugees-The Score, all soundtracks to my teenage years and beyond. And I was also gifted with a ticket to Janet Jackson's All For You tour, 9th row for my 18th birthday! A tour I still watch time to time, based on her party record of the same name.

There was also music playing at my various parties during games like "pass the parcel," "musical chairs", and one year, a dance competition. From the demos on the small Casio keyboard I had, 80's radio, and cassette tapes of Bollywood and Spanish music. One time, I even played classical music on piano for my sister's birthday party. I still associate all of those songs with innocent and carefree times. It makes processing my childhood memories on my "un-birthday" a lot easier.

Cont.

Getting so many presents, though most of them are no longer around, made me want to gift others with elaborate presents too. I recall buying a magnet making kit for one friend, shortly after I got a similar type of jewelry making kit for my 10th birthday, cause it was so much fun making creations and I wanted others to feel the same joy from creating art as I did. Another time, I bought a magic show set for my best friend. In my teens, I recall buying cassettes of Brandy's self-titled debut for my friend, Keith Sweat's self titled album for my cousin, and Spice Girl's Spice for my sister. All their songs entertained me well and I longed to share them with those who mattered to me most. It united us and having common interests empowered and motivated me, as well as getting out of my shell.

As an adult, I once got a musical cheesecake baked by a small business owner in my community. Pink and blue icing surrounded the fresh red strawberries, and brightly coloured musical notes were iced on the plate, after she saw a clip of me online singing Madonna's Borderline in my leather jacket. I can only imagine what other musical cakes I would get again someday. I associate the tastes and visual presentations with a time where I'm able to be present and endeavour the sugary tastes as I create good moments and more memories.

Also, my knack for choosing presents followed me in adulthood, sometimes. I now have a nephew and I hope to gift him with birthday presents soon, the way my uncle did for me, even when it wasn't my birthday. I loved playing board games with my mom as a kid, so I'm eyeing games like Candyland and Scrabble Jr. for him, so he's able to interact and learn at the same time outside of the classroom; colours, counting, reading and spelling. I'm also eyeing a pizza fractions game and the operation game for him at a later date, as well as children's books written by my friends, speaking of which, I wrote a children's short story for a publication recently and my aunt is going to share it with him. Moments like this are guided by empathy, and gratitude for the gifts and precious moments in life. I can only hope to make a positive difference in a child's well being, and also contribute to giving them memorable birthdays.

Musical Memories of a Bexley Girl
by
J. A. Newman

The first memory I have of any kind of music is of my nanna singing to me and rocking me on her lap. Songs such as 'Baa Baa Black Sheep' and 'We're two little sheep who've lost our way'. She also played the piano, 'The Teddy Bears' Picnic' and 'The Wedding of the Painted Doll'. I loved my dad playing the piano on a Sunday morning; the boogie-woogie and 'Walking my Baby Back Home' were my favourites. When I was seven he bought a Pye hi-fi in a polished walnut case and his first record, a ten-inch recording of Beethoven's symphony number 5 conducted by Otto Klemperer. The sixth and seventh symphonies followed along with recordings of Bach, Mozart and Vivaldi. My dad liked jazz too, names such as Fats Waller, Earl Hines and Louis Armstrong. When he was working on a piece of lettering in his studio he would listen to the third programme on the portable radio. We children had our own record player, a Portadyne. The first record I bought with my pocket money was an EP of The Temperance Seven for 11s 6d. I played it constantly. One track was called 'You're Driving Me Crazy' and as my mum said, it was very fitting!

I was about eight years old when I first saw Tommy Steele on the television. I loved his smile and his blond hair. When I was older I liked to watch *Wham!* and *Oh Boy* on Saturday tea-times where we were treated to Adam Faith, Marty Wilde and Cliff Richard.

Then came The Beatles. I bought every new release and stuck posters up in my bedroom, but I wasn't allowed to stick them on the wallpaper so I stuck them on every available surface I could: the fireplace, the wardrobe and the door. My dad liked The Beatles, he said their music was close to jazz with all the syncopated rhythms, and we used to listen together. I had a school friend whose father was in the police force who was given two tickets for a Beatles concert at the Lewisham Odeon in 1963. I was

Cont.

overjoyed. Wow! But I was very disappointed when the whole cinema was filled with screaming girls preventing me from hearing their music.

My dad took me to see West Side Story when I was 13 and I loved it so much that he bought me the sound track for Christmas. I took it to school to play in the music lesson; I wanted all my friends to fall in love with it too. I saw My Fair Lady, Mary Poppins and The Sound of Music. Most of these we saw whilst on holiday or at our local cinemas.

After going with a friend to the cinema to see Genghis Khan in 1966 I bought the sound track in our village music shop. I loved this music and my dad would listen with me and encourage my diverse tastes. Also in that year, I was introduced to our local jazz club at The Black Prince. I loved it. From then on I went every Monday evening with friends from work. We were treated to some of the big names like Kenny Ball and Chris Barber. Pop records were played during the break and this is when I got into Tamla Motown. 'Reach Out' by The Four Tops takes me straight back to those days. Sunday was R&B night when we had visiting bands such as The Shevelles, Gino Washington and the Ram Jam Band, The Ferris Wheel, The Amboy Dukes, Bonzo Dog and his Doo Dah Band, Traffic and Joe Cocker. It's only now that I realise how fortunate I was to be able to see all these live bands so close to home.

A Treasure, Lost Forever
by LaVern Spencer McCarthy

I gave birth to three, beautiful children, but I was only clairvoyant regarding my youngest son, Anthony. Before he was born, I dreamed that I had given birth to a white haired, blue-eyed son, which he was. He weighed almost eleven pounds at birth and only scored three on the APGAR scale, which is used to measure the well being of new-born babies. When he was three weeks old, he weighed fifteen pounds, and I could not carry him very far. He could empty a bottle of baby formula in about ten minutes. It seemed he was always hungry.

He was a good baby and slept through the night at three weeks, giving me a chance for much-needed rest. Tony, as we called him, was always happy and rarely ever cried. He was such a big baby he could wear his older brother's pants at one year of age if the legs were shortened. He had the sweetest smile. It made me think of the Gerber baby, with those rosy cheeks and impish smile.

I thought I had lost him a couple of times, once, when he unlatched the door and was able to go outside without me knowing.

We lived on a street where cars were zipping by constantly, and I was filled with terror, hoping he did not run in front of a moving vehicle. He was only a little older than one-year. I found him at a back yard swimming pool, looking into the water. The second time was when the older children were supposed to be watching him while I made a quick dash to the store. They weren't paying any attention to him, and when I walked back the way I had come, I saw a policeman holding Tony, and Tony was eating an ice cream cone. He had followed me. In both instances I cried tears of thankfulness that he was safe.

Tony had a good childhood, escaping the diseases children fell prey to in the past. Because of vaccinations, which were not available when I was a child, all three of my children grew up healthy and strong. My daughter, Angela married first and became

Cont.

the mother of three girls. My oldest son, Allen, married later, but never had children. His seven-year marriage ended in divorce. Tony was interested in the military and joined the National Guard at age eighteen. After that, he enlisted in the United States Army and was sent to Germany. He was there for two years, and I did not see him in person during that time.

When he returned to the states, he lived in Temple, Texas, not far from the Army base where he had been stationed. He was able to visit more often. He continued with his survey work and was doing well.

One night I saw him in a dream as he fell from somewhere above. He looked into my eyes as he passed before me. Not long after that he phoned and said while he was in Berlin, someone pushed him down the stairs from behind, and he broke both his ankles. He could not walk for weeks. I told him about my dream and he said, "Why didn't you tell me, and I would have avoided those stairs!"

Later on in life I had another dream, and I am sure it was prophetic. I saw Tony in a lake and he kept going away from me as I tried to follow him. Then the water turned to blood. When I awakened, I was shaken.

Time moved on, and Tony moved back closer to us and worked as a land surveyor. He would bring me antiques, such as old bottles and other items that he found in the fields. He enjoyed surveying, but later decided that he wanted to go to Louisiana and survey for the oil companies out in the Gulf of Mexico. He spent several years there and was exposed to many chemicals and gases. At one time, he lived in Metairie, Louisiana and worked in a surveying office. I had a chance to visit him while he lived there, and he showed me New Orleans. The Mardi Gras was in progress while I was there, and I was able to see the sights. He took me to a place that sold fresh oysters, and it was the first time I had ever been able to eat them. That was a few years after the hurricane, Katrina, came to town and upset so many lives. I saw people living in tents under bridges while I was there. They had no place else they could go.

One day I was walking across the floor of my home, and it struck me like a thunder bolt that Tony was going to die! *Oh, no I*

Cont.

thought, please tell me it is not so. But the feeling persisted, although at that time, Tony was healthy.

He married a lady named Rochelle later on. She was divorced and had four grown sons. One son, Matthew, lived with his mom and Tony. It was a happy household. Tony bought chickens to give the family eggs. He had a big rooster he called, King Henry. Something kept invading the chicken house, killing the chickens. King Henry was the last to go. No one could ever discover what was killing the chickens.

When Tony had been married for several years, he called me and told me he had found blood in his urine. He went to the doctor and they diagnosed kidney cancer. I have always thought it came from being around those chemicals when he worked in the Gulf. All I could say was, *oh no, oh no,* because I felt even then that Tony was going to die, although I would never tell him that.

He had surgery where the cancerous kidney was removed. He had a heart bypass at the same time. His recovery was rough, but he overcame the difficulties and resumed every day life, He was very optimistic about the future. He never resumed work but lived on disability.

When he, Rochelle and Matthew visited me, Tony took his shirt off, and he had a vivid scar that started below his neck and ended where the band of his trousers were. I hated to see that. It looked like someone had zipped him up from top to bottom. He gained a lot of weight, not like the many cancer victims I have known who were thin from the disease. The cancer showed no signs that it had returned, and everyone in the family breathed a little easier. Tony and I talked to each other frequently on the phone. We were very close and could tell each other our problems.

My husband died of kidney cancer also, in 2006. My daughter died from heart failure the next year. I was alone in the world except for Tony and Allen. Although I missed my daughter and husband, things weren't too bad when I still had my sons. Allen came to live with me since he was divorced from his second wife. He has been a comfort to me, going out of his way to help.

I continued to correspond with Tony and Rochelle although we could not visit each other as much as we would like. Three years after his diagnosis of cancer, he was told it had returned. We were all stricken with fear.

Cont.

I hoped against hope that something could be done to save him, but cancer is insidious. I feel that once it is in a person's body, it can strike again at any moment. This time there was no way the doctors could remove another kidney, so they resorted to medicine, which did little good. A few months later, Tony became mostly bedfast, although he was able to move around enough to sit in a chair. We talked a lot on the phone since we lived far apart.

Tony's doctors finally decided he needed surgery to remove a cancerous tumor. They operated, but they could not get near the tumor. In my opinion they cut him up for no reason because the tumor had spread all over his body. But I am not a doctor, and it is only my personal thoughts about this tragedy.

Tony was sent home to die. Hospice was a great help and comfort to him and Rochelle. I always held out hope for his recovery, but it was not to be. The child I had raised was dying, and not one thing could be done about it except try to make him comfortable and give him all the love and consideration that was possible. Rochelle was with him all the way. Each time he had to be in the hospital, she was always there, never leaving him alone.

Rochelle told us that if it was possible, we needed to visit Tony. Allen borrowed an SUV to take us that long way to Louisiana. I can't describe the look on Tony's face when we walked in the door. Rochelle had kept our visit as a surprise.

We stayed for about a week because we had to return the borrowed vehicle. During our stay, we had many conservations with Tony, Rochelle and Matthew. Rochelle took me to the fish market and bought shrimp which she cooked the Cajun way, and it was delicious.

We went to a store and made Tony a care basket since it was almost Easter.

Allen and I went to a park beside Lake Pontchartrain while we were there. We saw the remains of a sugar mill that had been abandoned long ago. Most of the trees were covered with moss. There was a pier that went over part of the lake, and we walked

Cont.

to the end of it. Everything seemed unreal to me, like a dream I could not awaken from. Allen and I were very sad about Tony's condition. To hope was futile. We managed to look happy when we were around Tony, but it was hard. He tried to look cheerful too, but I know he was as terrified as we were. He was forty-eight years old, and life had dealt him a dirty blow.

It is horrible to know one is dying, and nothing can be done about it. I think it is one of the worst things that can befall a human being, that knowing, and fear of the unknown.

But Tony had faith in God, that everything would be all right, even though he was afraid. He died strong in his faith, and perhaps that made dying easier.

Saying goodbye to him because we had to go was one of the hardest things I ever had to do. We both knew we would never see each other again in life, but perhaps we would meet again in the hereafter.

I called him every day on the phone until he died. Ten days later Rochelle called us early in the morning and told us Tony was gone. She was devastated, as we all were. Much money had been raised by others to buy medicine for Tony while he lived, and his church gave a large amount for his burial.

After he died, my life became a void for a long time. To have one of the dearest people I ever knew, perish that way was heart breaking.

At least we got to spend one, last Easter together, and Tony's birthday was April 24th. He had a big birthday party with a birthday cake and lots of presents. Most of his friends as well as in-laws were at the party.

I hated to leave him, but we needed to go home. If we had known he would pass away so soon, we would have stayed. He was buried at a veteran's cemetery in Slidell, Louisiana. I wish we could have brought him to be buried in Texas where he was born, but it was impossible.

My daughter's and Tony's death have left such a void in my life. I think everything is okay and suddenly it hits me that those I loved the most are gone forever.

T
R
A
V
E
L

Holy Island
by
Heather Haigh

Driving over the Cymyran Strait, my spirit takes to the wing—a fitting response to my arrival on Holy Island. It may have been named after the many religious sites it boasts, but it's the sheer beauty that steals my breath.

I head for the Western side, dominated by Holyhead Mountain where the craggy faces of the hillsides are softened by swathes of lime green, deep olives, pinks, purples russets, and sprinklings of acid-bright yellow. A twisting, chunky limestone path leads me up to the Roman watchtower Cwer Y Twr, where the views entice me to stretch my arms and soar. A cerulean sky, broken only by wisps of brilliant white, is sprinkled with ebony ravens, chocolate and buff honey buzzards, and black-headed gulls.

To the South of the mountain, I wander amongst the Cytiau'r Gwyddelod - stone circles which are the remains of an Iron Age Celtic settlement. The area is as rich in flora as it is in history. I wander through a carpet of twinkling blue Sheep's Bit, frothy white heads of Wild Carrot, cerise and shocking pink Bell Heather. The pretty yellow flowers of the Kidney Vetch look as though they have been stuffed with teased cotton wool. Surprisingly enough, it's possible to spot Bog Pimpernel, the clusters of pink flowers growing in pockets where rainwater has collected. To my mind, no plant surpasses the Heath Spotted Orchids, their dense flower spikes resembling pink and purple moths partying in a cluster. To my mind, no plant surpasses the Heath Spotted Orchids, their dense flower spikes resembling pink and purple moths partying in a cluster. The tiny white flowers of eyebright, adorned with fine strokes of colour applied at the hand of a meticulous artist, transport me right into a Monet.

Cont.

Heading back towards the coast, grasses and wildflowers provide a fringe of jewelled colours set against the backdrop of a sapphire sea which sparkles with flecks of silver, as magical as Cinderella's ballgown. Sunshine yellow flowers of the South Stack Fleawort provide gorgeous contrast. Peering over the edge, I see slabs of grey granite, which the island has cast into the ocean with abandon, catching the sea and sending up white spumes of foam. The fresh tang of salt air is peppered with hints of sweetness and the silence broken only by the splashing of waves and the call of seabirds. I remember what it is to be alive.

Where the land flattens out I see glossy black birds, blood-red curved beaks giving them an appearance of wicked ferocity, jaunty red stockings adding to the shock of colour, my first sighting of Choughs and one I will long remember. I heard tell that when King Arthur met his bloody end, it was a Chough that carried his soul away. I can believe it.

The path up the Western shore is flanked by lacey white froths of cow parsley, studded with emerald green rose-chafer beetles, almost as big as my thumbnail. Their backs are iridescent, flecked with purples and bronzes, like oil on a puddle beneath a summer sky. I look closely, I can see their furry underbellies and the alien antennae sprouting from their heads. Beautiful, fascinating, little creatures that must surely have fallen from the stars.

The land curves out towards the sea, like a slumbering sea cow, the tapering snout nudging a small rock infant. I head past the tiny white castle which sits upon the cliff top and turns out to be Elin's tower—a **crenelated** Victorian folly, now an RSPB information centre devoted to the seabirds which I have come to watch on the cliffs at South Stack.
I thrill at the raucous screech and growling *caaarrrr* of the razorbills, the unmistakable white line running through their black bill and the distinctive matching plumage. Guillemots waddle like little penguins, making their excitable chirps, whistles, and coos. Look up, and watch a circling peregrine falcon. But the little guys I particularly came to look for, and spend ages combing the cliffs for the tantalising sight of, are the puffins.

Cont.

Their comically large colourful beaks make them the favourite of many. Spot one with a billful of small fish and the sight is even more adorable. Watching them take off and land is a comedic joy to behold.

Looking down on South Stack, the geometric shapes of the walls make a simple jigsaw of the land, the lighthouse standing white and proud. I follow the winding steps down to Stack Bridge, watching intently for seals or dolphins, but my luck is out.

Looking out to sea, I can see the faint silhouette of land shimmering in the pale pinky blue haze - perhaps I'm looking at the Lleyn Peninsula or Bardsey Island, other places I might visit someday. But for now, I plan to explore more of this gem of a place—a place where fairytales and follies meet antiquity and space-creatures.

The Rat Man of Edinburgh
by Hannah McIntyre

Edinburgh is known for a few things: home of whisky and tartan, a city rich with history and culture which hides a dark underbelly. Hundreds of years ago, Edinburgh's murky corners were avoided by residents and authorities alike due to the notorious meddling of witches and criminals. Today the city has changed, the laughing street performers juggling swords and cracking jokes are a far cry from the macabre scenes of the past. However, if you know where to go, or accidentally stumble upon it as I did, there are still places in Edinburgh where the mysticism of old meets contemporary bustle.

Almost a year ago now, I travelled alone to Edinburgh to stay in a cheap hostel for a few nights. I stayed in the middle of what's known as The Old Town of Edinburgh, it's a beautiful place, especially when I visited at the beginning of November as Christmas lights had begun to twinkle on every column and doorway.

One night in my bed I was restless, I couldn't stay in my shared dormitory and the woman on the bunk above me had made that abundantly clear with her angry shushing throughout the previous night. So, I decided to don my winter coat and step out into the icy chill of the Scottish air, to wander until my mind could at last come to rest.

It was a cold and drizzly night, typical of the Scottish weather, yet despite the miserable clime, I was enthralled by the bustle of the city so late at night. It must have been nearly midnight, but the city was alive. Teenagers crowded around the McDonalds clamouring for attention, cars and buses filled the roads zipping along quickly, only halting for the flashing lights of the police or ambulance services. I felt electric, invigorated by the scene which I was now a part of a lone traveller amidst the night. I kept walking, past the huge buildings ensconced in light, past the monuments whose shadows reached back for miles, past the activity of the main streets until I reached the base of Calton Hill.

Cont.

I had visited this place in the day, trekked to the top of the hill, walked its paths and marvelled at the many monuments which adorn its peak. It's a funny place, Calton Hill. It holds up a Scottish mimicry of classic Roman design whilst also offering the most perfect views of the city from every angle, a quiet place where one can be pensive and reflect. In the day, I had appreciated all its glories, so at night I sought it as a refuge for my tumultuous emotions.

The climb to the peak was short and the route was lined by a row of stairs which ascend steeply upwards. However, at this time of night, the stairs were unlit. The light of the one lamp at the base offered a measly glow over the lower portion, sending the rest of the staircase running upwards into a black abyss. I could see no one around, but above me, I could hear strange noises like an occasional scream or disembodied cackle. I heard scuffing and shuffling but there was no light and no bodies to be seen. I ascended slowly, unusually drawn to the summit, feeling the pull of some intangible force within the place.

What was up there? Who knows. Could it be the conjurings of some old magic which still lingered in this shadowy city? Or was it merely a group of kids or crackheads roaming wild and free in this less frequented portion of the night-held city. I was afraid to see the gormless faces of those smacked up on drugs trudging like zombies through the dark as they stumble into each other and groan through the tendrils of narcotic smoke. I was perhaps equally afraid of the teenagers who often carry knives and no remorse, unhindered by adult perceptions of the world and untamed by convention. The teenagers are unpredictable, they may not care one wink about your presence, or they may find it a crime punishable by their own immoral laws. Yet, what I was certainly most afraid of was something much older and much more dangerous, something unrestrained by the bounds of natural law, the infamous witches of Edinburgh. There aren't many places left in the UK where the veil between the supernatural and the natural remains so thin, thousands of years of bloodshed not destroyed or banished has merely been built over, leaving liminal places where the two worlds can collide.

Cont.

Despite the allure of ascending to the top of the hill and discovering its nighttime secrets, I felt more compelled to stay near the bottom. Young women are taught to fear the mysterious figures in the dark from a young age, especially when alone in an unfamiliar city when no one knows exactly where you are, not even yourself. I climbed a few steps, remaining within the glow of the streetlight and sat down, producing a bottle of wine from my small bag. I began sipping in the hopes of finding a weariness which could finally carry me off to sleep. Time passed, and so did a few random pedestrians, regular people passing by on their way home after a long night. They hardly noticed me, hardly cared. Only one man spoke to me. Was he a man? I can't be entirely sure. Whatever he was, he appeared before me in a human form.

Whilst sitting on the steps, everything around me fell quiet save for the ceaseless noises from the top of the hill which acted as a permanent eerie soundtrack, a warning not to go any further up. I hadn't seen any creatures all night, not a pigeon nor a dog, or a cat, nothing. Suddenly a huge rat appeared from around the corner at the base of the stairs. It ran decisively up towards me, winding itself around the handrail and squeaking as it went. I stood up lest it ran across my lap and moved from its path, disgusted that I had been sitting upon a place frequented by vermin. Distracted by my own loathing, I failed to recognise the flurry of rats which appeared from the around the same corner at the bottom of the stairs until they were all rushing up towards me chittering as they ran. Then I heard something louder, an unreal scream which cut through the darkness. Perhaps not a scream but a growl, certainly inhuman, a guttural throaty noise unlike anything I had ever heard a creature of the natural earth make. It bellowed through the darkness with keening intonations, it appeared to me that it was instructing the rats, goading them into running towards me. Instinctively, I backed away. Suddenly my fear of what may be atop the hill seemed insignificant compared to what lay below. I stumbled backward up the stairs, not daring to tear my eyes from the scene before me. Never turn your back on danger. The rats came closer, as did the sound. I knew that at any moment

Cont.

would beast emitting the growl would round the corner, the tension of the moment was crescendoing to its inevitable climax.

It was a man, an ordinary man. Wearing simple tracksuit bottoms and a windbreaker, his face looked clean and smooth, not crinkled and distorted like that of a drug addict. He appeared to me entirely normal. The noise stopped immediately as he rounded the corner. He looked up at me as I continued to make my way up the stairs, eyeing him suspiciously, afraid of his next attack.

"You don't have to run away." He laughed light-heartedly as if he was in on a joke that I wasn't. "I was just talking to the rats."

I couldn't respond, couldn't move. Without the encouragement of his inhuman cry, the rats had dissipated quickly, leaving me and him alone in the orange lamplight and shadows. I was shocked by the normalcy of his voice, certainly mismatched to the sound he had made moments before which was low and warbling; his speaking voice was quite high-pitched and melodic. I stood still waiting for him to pass, and for some time after that too. When I was sure he must be gone I ran from the place, hurrying back to the safe confines of my shared dormitory where the sleeping bodies felt safe and where a man at reception sat up all night to keep us from harm.

A Place Less Visited
by
Julie Watson

Among my friends, the plain speaking ones would be quick to point out that I am not blessed with an especially good sense of direction. Unfortunately, it's true. I only feel geographically confident on the patch of the planet that my feet are most familiar with; my home turf, which is the area roughly within a half a mile circumference of my house.

As I'm a travel writer, you would think that being navigationally-challenged might be a bit of an impediment. Surprisingly, however, despite many years of globe-trotting with just a tourist map in hand and some unhelpful phrases in the local language, I have rarely lost my way.

But 'rarely' is not the same as 'never'. There was one occasion, which I recall with some embarrassment. It took place early on in my travelling career and not in some wild uncharted corner of the world even if it did seem like the back of beyond. That I was lost somewhere in the hinterland of deepest Kent only became apparent during a routine conversation on a train. The memory of it is etched into my brain:

Raising my eyes from my book, I see green. The regulation standard issue waistcoat of a British Rail conductor. He has a leather satchel hanging off his shoulder and is wielding a heavy duty ticket punch.

"Tickets please"

I pass him a small rectangular piece of beige cardstock: a 1970s

Cont.

railway ticket permitting me to travel from London to Dover down down on the south coast even if its print is barely legible. It is silently scrutinised for a moment then handed back to me with a damning pronouncement.

"Yer on the wrong train, luv"

My eyes travel up from the green waistcoat to the face of the conductor.

Uncomprehending, I continue, "I'm going to Dover – to catch the night ferry." I somehow expect this information will help him change his statement.

"This train don't stop there. We'll be endin' in Faversham, luv."

I have never heard of Faversham: it's 1976, I am in my early twenties and my geographical ignorance knows no bounds. But I do know I'm on my way back to Paris where I am spending a year as a language assistant in a French lycée as part of my degree course. I've been home to England for a flying visit which has terminated in a late night out with friends in the clubs and pubs of London. This was followed by a mad dash across London to reach Victoria station in time to catch the last train to Dover for the night ferry. I was lucky, I barely made it through the ticket barrier in time, leaping into the nearest train carriage just as the guard was raising the whistle to his lips.

So here I am, on the 23.40 train from London Victoria bound for the cross channel ferry terminal. In the morning I should be in Calais and by mid-morning tomorrow, Paris - or so I thought until a moment ago.

Cont.

The conductor regards me curiously while I try to understand what has happened. After a few questions it becomes clear that my athletic leap at Victoria station landed me on the wrong train, one with a final stop that falls disappointingly short of the English south coast and Dover.

Faversham, it turns out, is a small market town, not renowned for anything that might draw the occasional visiting tourist and, therefore, without a single B&B or hotel to its credit. And since the station is an insignificant stop on the Kent line and resembles more of a place for parking trains overnight, there is, unfortunately, not even a platform waiting room. There I could have passed the night until a train going all the way through to Dover arrived the next day. I only later learn that Faversham is mentioned in the Doomsday Book – information that might have struck me as somewhat ironic on that particular night back in 1976, had I known it then.

I have finally grasped the fact that I am not, as I'd hoped, on the 23.40 train to Dover. The conductor pulls out a dog-eared copy of the British Rail timetable from his satchel and consults it for several minutes, flipping back and forth between its pages. I watch him, biting my lip.

Finally he slaps the book shut, saying, " Leave it with me, luv." And with that, he moves on to complete his final ticket clipping of the night. I have no choice but to sit and stare out into the black Kentish night as the train trundles on towards the unknown Faversham.

An hour and a quarter later, we arrive at 00.57. I am fifty miles south of London but still eighteen short of my goal in Dover. The conductor opens the carriage door and we step out onto Faversham's empty platform. Apart from the driver, we are the last of the train's occupants to get off at the end of the line.

Cont.

I would like to be able to say that I then found an alternative mode of transport to reach the ferry terminal in time to catch my night crossing: a taxi perhaps, a pillion ride on the back of a motorbike or I would even have settled for a lift with a passing a horse and cart, but it was not to be.

The next morning I wake with slight neckache but otherwise rested despite some strange dreams. I am lying on a sofa wrapped in a blanket and there's a fireplace in front of me, no longer emitting any warmth although it was when I fell asleep. Above the mantelpiece, I see what I failed to notice last night. A large framed picture of a steam engine is bearing down towards me enshrouded in clouds of billowing white steam. I am still in Faversham and in the family home of Doug, the conductor, who, besides verifying that passengers' ticket destinations match with their choice of train, takes his responsibility for overseeing the safety and orderly transport of all passengers on British Rail very seriously.

His wife registered no surprise at all last night when I followed him sheepishly into their terraced house, a short walk from the station. Little was said and Doug turned in after confirming the arrangements for the following morning with me:

"Best get up early tomorrow, luv. Then we can put yer on the milk train. It comes through Faversham at 5.30"

The milk train? This was the train that ran very early each morning to bring milk into the towns and cities, Doug informed me. It was later replaced by road transport but luckily for me the milk train also carried passengers back in the 1970s.

Cont.

And so it is agreed. I will travel with the milk on to Dover in time to catch the first channel crossing of the day. I am left in the capable hands of his wife, who comes into the front living room with a blanket and pillow. I gather I'll be sleeping on the sofa but first she takes a pair of tongs and adds two lumps of coal to the dwindling fire. It is now very late so she goes out closing the door behind her to join her husband upstairs, and presumably to interrogate him as to who the woman on the sofa is. I fall asleep wrapped in the blanket, watching small animated flames dance above the grate and hoping that there will not be any marital strife on my account.

But the next morning, Mrs Doug – I never learned her name - waves me off with a smile from the front door when I leave with her husband for Faversham railway station in the early hours.

As I board the milk train on the next part of my round-about journey back to France, I thank Doug profusely, and apologise for any domestic upset I may have caused in his household.
He gives a shrug before replying, "Not t' worry, luv. We're getting used to visitors. See, yer not the first to make a mistake with the trains. A couple of months back, we 'ad two Japanese sleeping on our sofa."

The Fifteen Minute Tourist Escape
by
Meredith Stephens

It's easy to overlook tourist sites close to home in contrast to places at a great distance. Alex and I have traveled for many hours by car, boat and plane to exotic distant clines. We have sailed from Adelaide to New Caledonia and back, and driven from California to Utah. Recently we have found equal pleasure taking our dog for a walk in a nearby gorge. The Sturt Gorge is located at a fifteen minute drive from home in Adelaide, South Australia. Surely there would be no tourist spots awaiting us so close to home?

There are a number of entry points to the Sturt Gorge, which borders suburbia. You can walk straight into the gorge from a number of streets, so there is no sense of a grand arrival. We parked our car opposite some houses, and entered the gate to walk down the hill into the gorge. Alex took Haru, our border collie, grasping the end of her bright red leash. She jumped out of the car, wondering where we were going to take her that day. We descended past the spring bottle brushes and gum trees until we found the creek with stepping stones. In winter the stepping stones are submerged and the stones are slippery, so occasionally we have had to abandon our walk there.

Cont.

This time the stepping stones were peaking above the water line and we skipped across, followed by Haru. At least half of the pleasure of this walk was vicarious. Haru wanted to stop and sniff the ground every few metres but we impatiently tugged her along. We kept looking for a giant log which had fallen over the creek which we had noticed in winter. A couple were coming towards us in the opposite direction cradling their dog in their arms.

"You'll have to pick up your dog! It's treacherous," they warned us.

Haru is on the small side for a border collie but still too heavy to pick up, so we could not heed the couple's advice. There were six creek crossings on the route we had chosen, but thankfully the stepping stones were dry on each crossing. Haru confidently and proudly trotted across the stepping stones. We released her from the lead for the crossings in case she inadvertently dragged us into the creek. Sometimes she crossed the creek ahead of us, looked back to check on us, returned to us, and then crossed the creek again, in total for about five times in the time it took for us to step across the creek ourselves.

We spotted a giant log strewn across the creek, but it looked slightly different from the one we remembered from our winter hike, so we continued along the banks of the creek, clambering across rocks, placing our feet strategically to avoid slipping into the creek. After criss-crossing the creek four times we spotted the giant log crossing the creek that we had noticed before. We released Haru to witness her racing across the log on her dainty paws.

Cont.

The final part of the walk was the most challenging. It had been easy descending into the gorge, but in order to complete the loop we had to clamber up a steep incline. I complained to Alex in my typical fashion, and he continued to encourage me. I placed one foot in front of the other, stopping every now and then to catch my breath. Finally we arrived at the top of the gorge, and walked in the shade of the gum trees, on a path bordering suburbia, back to the car.

I congratulated myself that we could travel a short distance, without having to leave our dog behind, any time we wanted, to complete a mildly challenging walk in the shade to the sound of running water. This is not to detract from exotic holidays in far-flung corners of the globe, but it is reassuring to know that we can indulge in an escape in a nearby location that few have heard of. My visits to far flung locations such as the sail to New Caledonia, and the drive from California to Utah coloured my view of this local walk and I was able to appreciate it anew. As Alain de Botton reminded us: "Home all at once seems the strangest of destinations, its every detail relativized by the other lands one has visited".

Quick Reads

That's His Boy
by Con Chapman

We had finished up at the Bagby place and I thought we were through for the day but Ronnie and Jim said no, we had one more job to do.

"It's almost dark," I said. I didn't know if you could rig up a light on the truck and bale hay at night that way, but I'd had enough.

"It's a little job, a piss ant farm," Ronnie said. "We'll do it quick and get paid extra."

"Why—is it supposed to rain tomorrow?" I asked. I knew some farmers would pay you more if they needed to get their hay in the barn before it rained.

"Naw, the guy's rich," Jim said. "He's payin' us extra because he can afford it."

We were almost back into town, at the five-way stoplight by the cemetery. Instead of going straight to my house, or the left fork back to Ronnie's house, Jim took a hard left, past the Holiday Inn out towards where the new subdivision was going in.

We went past the country club and turned into a driveway that led to a new house. I recognized it because it had been a farm when I was growing up; our neighbors knew the people who lived there, we went out there to ride an old horse one time.

The house that used to be there was just a farm house; the new one was a fancy suburban one, although there was still a barn out back. A man came out to greet us on a tractor; he had a teenage boy riding behind him on back.

Cont.

"Glad you all could make it, follow me out back," the man said. He turned the tractor around and headed out behind the house where there was a field of baled hay to be taken in.

"See, it ain't so much," Ronnie said. It was still work, but I could tell it wasn't going to be that hard, maybe three truckloads. Still, I would have rather been home.

The boy got down and came over to where we were so that there four of us working; two bucking the bales, Ronnie on the truck bed stacking them, Jim driving. The boy didn't say much, just smiled a goofy smile and said "Let me help" after he jumped off the tractor and came over.

"You take the left side," I said. I'm right-handed, so it was easier for me to be on that side. Once we got goin' I could tell the boy was right-handed too; he had to turn around to sling the bales on the truck going against him, which slowed him down as the motion of his swing carried him away from the truck as it rolled through the field.

The kid slowed us down but after a while I just ignored him; I figured he'd get the hang of it and any help would get the job done quicker. He was fatter than all of us and wasn't really prepared. He wore just a white t-shirt; I liked to wear sleeves so my arms don't get all scratched up—besides, it was getting cool as the sun went down. His gloves were cotton-like and didn't look like they were going to last long. I learned to get leather gloves the hard way, the first day Ronnie and Jim took me out. My hands were so cut from the twine the first morning I could barely hoist a bale by noontime. The farmer gave me a set of his gloves when we broke for lunch and I made it to the end of the day.

Cont.

We got the truck loaded and I got in the cab with Ronnie and Jim. The boy got on the back of the tractor again and rode back to the barn with the man.

We got the first load into the barn without much trouble; the loft wasn't big, I guess because the man didn't have that much land. You didn't have to haul the bales very far across the floor, me and the boy would just grab them off the loader, turn around and stack them.

We didn't talk much while we were working in the loft; at one point the boy asked me if I played football and I said yes.

"I'm going out this year," he said with a big grin on his face, as if I was supposed to be impressed.

"Is that so?" I said and just kept working.

"I'm trying to get in shape. I've heard it's tough."

"First week is hell," I said. I didn't want to seem soft, but I figured a guy like him would just waste everybody's time going out. Might as well try and discourage him.

When we were done the boy rode out to the field on the back of the tractor like before. I guessed it was only going to take one more run, and by the time we got out to where the man's property ended I could see it wasn't even going to be a full load. We made the turn and headed back towards the barn; there was still maybe fifty bales scattered around to get.

"I'm goin' in—nice to meet you," the boy said as he ran off and hopped on the back of the tractor. I looked at Ronnie but his face didn't even change, like the loss of one pair of hands was no big deal. Of course it wasn't to him, he was stacking, not bucking.

The boy caught up with the tractor and hopped on behind, like before. What would have been an easy finish was now twice as hard, and I resented it.

"What's up with him?" I yelled up to Ronnie.

"I guess that's all he's gonna do—you can finish up, we're almost done."

I wouldn't have minded ordinarily, but for the kid to just pick up and leave like that made me mad.

"Who the hell is he?" I shouted at Ronnie.

"That's his boy," he said, nodding off towards the tractor.

"He don't have to work, you do, so get busy."

Memory
by
Barbara Hull

Everyone used to say quite cruelly that Amy had been "left on the shelf", a term used often in that post-war era when so many of the nation's youth had been cruelly mown down in the 1914-18 war. In sheer practical terms, those returning from the Great War were just too few to satisfy the needs of women of marriageable age. Those who did not succeed in landing a husband were referred to as "old maids". Not the prettiest of girls, Amy had resigned herself to "old maidship" and concentrated on being a first-rate maiden aunt.

She spoilt her nephews unashamedly took the eldest, twelve-year-old Anthony, on holiday with her to Blackpool. In the boarding house dining room she caught the eye of an older man, holidaying alone. He struck up a conversation as he passed her the cruet and they clicked straight away. He soon discovered Amy's marital status and charmed her with all the delights on offer at Blackpool, the Pleasure Beach, the Tower Ballroom, the landau rides.

It soon emerged that both Amy and Fred were from Preston and they arranged to meet again. Amy had never been a great lover of dances, usually ending up as a wallflower but Fred was an excellent dancer, gave her some private lessons and took her to the Conservative Club dances. They were quite the stars on the dance floor and she felt like a princess. Her head was well and truly turned and contrary to her brother John's advice, at the age of forty Amy, the old maid, married her Fred, the sophisticated older man, knowing precious little about him. Within two years, after a brief illness, he died of cancer but those two years were sufficient to provide Amy with a much needed boost to her status, no longer an old maid left on the shelf, she almost enjoyed the higher status afforded by saying, "I'm a widow."

In addition she had her treasure store of memories of the good times they had shared before his illness had snatched him away.

As the years passed, her memories became rosier and a source of great joy in her silver years, her two years with Fred acquiring an intensity almost on a par with Abelard and Eloise, Romeo and Juliet, Napoleon and Josephine…

Cont.

John had always despaired of his sister's gullibility and had kept an eye out for "our Amy" since childhood. She had always been a pushover for a compliment and really did need to be liked. He felt sorry for her never having a boyfriend especially as her sister, Bella, had never been short of admirers but as Amy always admitted, "Bella was always the pretty one."

So, when she returned from Blackpool babbling about her suitor, he was worried she might be exploited. Meeting Fred, he was slightly relieved, interpreting his behaviour as paternalistic, rather than predatory. He was, after all over twenty-five years' older than Amy, and retired. He shared a converted semi-detached house his married son, occupying the ground floor while the young couple lived upstairs.

The proposed marriage had come as quite a shock to John. Fred was already retired but Amy was still working in the biscuit factory and quite enjoyed it, even more now she had the enhanced status of being married. Fred explained to her that he and his son were buying this house together and that they paid fifty per cent each on the mortgage. Amy readily agreed to pay her and Fred's half from her wages. After all, he always had a nice meal ready for her when she arrived home from work. Amy was paid in cash and passed on the appropriate amount for their share of the mortgage every Friday. She was deliriously happy with her new status.

When they had been married about a year, Fred's son, Clive and his wife decided to emigrate to Canada on an assisted passage, but said they would keep sending Fred their share of the mortgage as it would be an insurance should they want to come back to the old country if things did not work out.

When they had been gone several months Fred was suddenly taken ill and Amy gave up her job at the biscuit factory to nurse him through what was to prove a terminal illness. She phoned the couple in Canada who protested that

Cont.

they could not afford to return for the funeral which Amy paid for from her own somewhat meagre savings.

Gwen, Amy's sister-in-law, helped to sort out the paperwork Fred had always kept in an old biscuit tin in the kitchen cupboard and they found a joint mortgage agreement between Fred and his son stating that, in the event of the death of either borrower, the deeds of the property would pass to the other borrower. Gwen asked, "Did Fred never make a will for you to inherit?"

It appeared that the question had never been broached. Gwen had to spell it out, "It means that the house now belongs totally to Clive."

Amy was very defensive, "I'm sure he meant to. He just never got round to it."

Gwen telephoned Canada, "Don't worry" said Clive, "We won't see Amy homeless. Just tell her to keep up the mortgage payments"

John and Gwen thought this was a terrific cheek and they persuaded Amy to leave the house and move in with them till she got a flat of her own.

What they could not bear to tell her was that the mortgage paying in book they had found in the biscuit tin showed that the ten pounds fifteen shillings a month Amy had been paying was in fact the total monthly payment, not the half share Fred had told her.

"Let sleeping dogs lie," said big brother John, "They certainly took our Amy for a ride, didn't they? But she has some wonderful memories."

"You're right," said Gwen, "Who'd want to take that away? It's all she's got."

A Flower By Any Other Name.
by
Michael Shawyer

"But I saw him bury you."

Petunia stared at her gravel-faced brother. "I am sorry to disappoint you Gary but whoever you saw, it wasn't me."

"It was. Your hair, your clothes. On my life."

"Well please explain dear brother how I am standing here when according to you I should be six feet under?" Gary shook his head but the cobwebs in his drug-addled brain only spun tighter. He was off his head and wouldn't remember a thing tomorrow.

Another voice came from the kitchen. "So did I."

Gary's two-faced drug-addict girlfriend with more lies on the tip of her tongue than a prime minister and Petunia sighed. Her busy evening had just got busier. *Could the pair of them be sharing an hallucination?* Whatever the reason, there would be no quick way out with Julie the Junky involved. It was time Petunia decided - these two were overdue a sorting.

"Julie, what a surprise. You do know it's nine o'clock? You're usually on your back in the park with a queue stretched to the gates. What do you think you saw?"

"Everyfin."

"Everything?"

"Yeah. You're a vampire, rising up from the grave. You better pay up or we'll tell the cops." Julie's acid-charged mind buzzing and Petunia thrust her face in close. The junkie backing away and colliding with the television. "Ouch. Hey, that's assault that is."

Cont.

Here, take my phone. Call the police. I hear they want to talk to you. Something about mugging one of your punters?" The addict looked down at her mud-caked trainers. *How the f**k does she know that? Gary! Of course it was.* Her fellow mugger opened his mouth more often than Julie opened her legs and she backtracked.

"Sorry, sorry - my mistake. Didn't see nuffin' don't know nuffin'. God's my witness."

Petunia grabbed her throat. Forefinger and thumb encircling the windpipe. Squeezing. Her painted nails punctured the skin and Gary scrunched himself in a ball. Pulling a woollen hat over his ears and eyes. A tinnitus of humming whistled through the gaps in his teeth.

"Die bitch." Petunia's patience had run out and she squeezed harder. Blood trickling over her fingernails. This was overdue and she enjoyed the final moments. A tremor passing through her groin when Julie's lights went out.

"Get up." Petunia kicked her brother.

"Leave me alone. Nothing to do with me. Didn't see anything. Don't know nuthin'. No comment."

"Shut up and get the f**k up." She pulled his arms from around his head.

"What?"

"Pick up Julie and follow me."

"What's wrong with her?"

"Sleeping."

Cont.

"Urrr! She stinks, she's shit herselff!"

"Of course she has. She's a junky." Petunia closed her ears to his complaints and opened the front door. "Follow me and keep up."

It was less than a hundred yards to the shopping mall where she kept her secrets under the guise of a costume hire shop. Halfway across the goods yard Gary stumbled and the corpse flopped on the tarmac. He was still bent double when Petunia kicked him.

"You clumsy, useless prat. Pick her up." She took an arm. Between them dragging the body in the stockroom. It was wall to wall with fancy dress outfits. The Halloween masks moving in the breeze teased Gary's fractured nerves.

"Get hold of her. Up on the table." Julie's head clunked against the edge and Gary apologised. "Sorry babe, sorry."

Petunia turned on her brother, "Come on. Get moving."

"Look at her. She don't look too good." Gary chewing his knuckles.

"You're right, she doesn't."

"We should get a doctor, go to casualty. They know us there."

"Too late."

"Too late?"

"Yes Gary. Too late. She's dead."

"Dead?" Gary's knees gave way and he hit the concrete floor with a clunk.

Cont.

"Yes. Dead, and the police will think you did it."

"Huh? Why?"

"Because I'll tell them it was you."

"But I didn't."

"Well my dear brother who are they going to believe? Her junky boyfriend or a local businesswoman?"

"Tooney, Tooney please don't tell them." Gary reverting to her childhood nickname. "Please. I'll do anything."

"Anything?"

His answer was lost in a burst of sobbing.

"Stop crying." Petunia slapped her brother. "What did you say?"

"Yes. Yes. I said yes."

"Wipe your nose." An industrial chest freezer was alongside the table and Petunia raised the lid. "Put her in there."

"Whaaat? She'll freeze to death."

"She's already dead. That's what they do with dead people." The confusion and drugs were too much and Gary shut down. After a moment pushing Julie across the table and into the freezer. She snagged. Half in and half out.

"Stuck Tooney. Julie's stuck."

"Well get on the table and *unstick* her." A knock at the door made them both jump.

Cont.

"Cops! Quick Gary. Hide in the freezer."

"She's sticking up. There's something underneath."

"Hurry the f**k up." Gary was on all fours and she shouldered him on top of the corpse. "Get down."

He flopped on top of Julie and Petunia hammered his backside with the lid.

"Can't Tooney. Can't. Julie's elbow."

Petunia raised the lid to its full height and slammed it down. Sighing when the catch clicked. The door rattled again.

"Coming," and she dashed across the warehouse.

"Evening Ma'am." The mall security guard touched his cap. "Saw your light on. Wanted to make sure all is OK."

"Thanks Grozdan. Only me. Burning the midnight oil as usual."

"No worries." The guard tapped his nose with a finger and winked. "No piece for da wicket."

Petunia grinned and spun from the door. Racing across the warehouse and dragging her desk to one side. Revealing a trapdoor. She raced along the underground passage to her secret apartment.

Petunia portrayed herself as Daisy the Dominatrix on TikTok and within moments the transformation was complete. Cat-woman mask, PVC swimming costume, fishnet stockings and thigh-high boots. A whip clutched in her hand.

Someone had entered the private elevator that served her floor. The whir of the lift-motor stopping with a muted clunk and the twin doors slid apart. She cracked the whip, "Good evening Chief Constable. Whose been a naughty boy then?".

Meandering Intermittent Revolutions
by
Linda Hibbin

'Why you can't use the bus beats me,' Beth's beloved groused as she mounted her new 1980s Rayleigh Cameo.

'Too unreliable.' *Like you,* she thought, recalling his deplorable timekeeping when she occasionally asked him to chauffeur her to appointments or collect her from work.

'Get moving. It's cold.'

It was late evening. Nobody in sight. *Thank you, God.*

'Mind the wing mirrors,' Beth's beau roared as she wobbled close to cars parked nose to bumper. She jolted to a halt at the end of the road, her boobs sore from repeatedly slamming on the brakes.

'I want stabilisers,' the young woman blubbed, teetering with one foot on the tarmac. The spinning pedals struck her bruised legs, her bum hurt, and her elbows and knees scaped raw from recent tumbles.

'Jesus wept,' hubby hissed as Beth walked the bike around the corner. After enduring weeks of practice, she still couldn't turn corners despite His Lordship's plethora of unhelpful advice.

Mummy-dearest scoffed. She'd biked everywhere in her youth. 'Perhaps you'd be better off on four wheels,' she commented, unaware that Beth had collided with a metal hoarding and written off their car while the light of her life was teaching her to drive.

When Romeo recovered his sense of humour, he joked about the 'incident' to everyone. Demoralised, Beth bought a Honda scooter and sold it a week later. It was too fast, and she felt unsafe. However, it left her wondering if a pushbike would show more

Cont.

consideration, so she purchased the Cameo.

She'd never ridden a bicycle, but it looked easy, and she imagined skimming along country lanes with the wind in her hair until she cut across the path of a tractor and pedalled into a hedged bend.

Lover-boy insisted his missus become a proficient rider closer to home. Beth practised in the Supermarket car park when it had closed but became intimidated by the security guy shouting advice.

Beth's consort insisted she practice on the road outside their house, and he created a convenient timetable. He had missed too many televised football matches, and if he didn't need to drive Beth and the bike anywhere, he could have a drink.

Nocturnal wobble-abouts accomplished nothing.

Effortlessly steering a U-turn, Beth sold the bike, 'almost new,' and ditched her lesser half, surplus to requirements.

She took driving lessons and found an instructor with nerves of steel.

Eventually, Beth learned to drive and passed the driving test, although she wrote off her canary-yellow Fiat the first year.

She doggedly continued her unsteady road trip.

There was a smattering of minor 'incidents' in the following years, rewarded with 'points' on or off her licence; she wasn't sure which. Then the wing mirrors of stationary vehicles began to wallop hers as she motored past in granny gear. She didn't stop to check the damage to her vehicle or the ones that had assaulted her car. For goodness' sake, they were only wing mirrors. Easy to replace, and what could anyone expect with the damn things sticking out into the road?

Cont.

Her son good-naturedly replaced the broken mirrors on her car. Then, he began to worry about his mother's spatial awareness. Or lack of it.

When Beth's car developed a minor problem, he lied through his teeth and said it was becoming a hazard ('Not as big a hazard as Mum,' he told his brother.) and insisted she sold it while it was still worth something.

So.

Beth sold the car and purchased a mobility scooter.

Her sons expected Mum to buy a neat, lightweight model and were dismayed when they saw what she had chosen. As far as they were concerned, she was more trouble than their teenage kids.

Beth's newest form of transport was a mean machine with large wheels and a comfortable, adjustable captain's seat. It was an all-terrain beast that could scale steep hills, ride over sands, go fast and far and was permitted on the road.

Beth felt thirty years younger in her new leather gear, flying along the road with the wind in her hair. Overtaking parked vehicles was not a problem, and …

best of all …

It was, indeed, easy.

Three Flash Fiction Stories from Christopher T. Dabrowski

Searching for Alien Civilisations

We sent radio signals into space, hoping to contact an alien civilisation.

Unfortunately, for decades no one responded.

The universe seems dead, but we know how it is - with such unimaginable distances, it can take thousands of years before a signal reaches a recipient.

We could extinct before that happens.

It arrived faster, passing through several space-time curves, and damaged alien vehicles - their structure was so different that the radio signal was like a laser.

Enraged, the aliens carried out complex calculations and targeted Earth.

They came to exact bloody revenge for the "terror act" carried out by the Earthlings.

Sneaky Planet Takeover

Wars, viruses, environmental disasters, and subsequent economic collapse. It led to a world government and a top-down planned scarcity economy.

People got a guaranteed income - barely enough to survive.

They couldn't save - digital money had a limited expiry date, vanishing beyond its use-by date.

We monitor people with nanobot chips injected as vaccines - we decide who gets sick and to what.

We also screen their brains to know what's on someone's mind.

    Few still travel - cars are a luxury.

Only chosen few outside the system can afford it.

    The earth is ours - and now, it's time to chemically disrupt fertility.

The Real Reason for Postponing the First Date

I persuaded her to meet for a long time.

Once our date happened, I understood her reluctance.

She looked phenomenal, but normal, in the photos. She changed her skin color.

Now she stood in front of me, blue.

    The purple on her cheeks showed that she was blushing.

    - Relax, you're beautiful. I like it. Blue is sensual.

    - Really? - she stares at me intently, probing whether I'm saying this out of pity.

But I tell the truth.

    Poor girl, she probably went through a lot at school.

    - Parents... were fans of that movie from three centuries ago, she explains.

    - Avatar?

    - Yes.

1912
by D C Diamondopolous

"Women and children first! Women and children first!"

A brandy snifter in one hand, a cigar in the other, I am alone as I watch people rush about on deck from the comfort of my leather chair in the first-class smoking room. It's past midnight, the lights flicker, but I am ruthlessly serene, for I did not overcome my childhood in the slums of the East End to drown in the freezing Atlantic water.

Second-class is where I belong, but who's to care now? When faced with death, we're all in the same boat.

Perhaps you've heard of me, Julian Grey, or seen my name on music hall marquees from Belfast to London.

I've made an enviable living as a comic, mimic, dancer, and acrobat. But what has brought me my greatest fame, and why I set sail on the Titanic to New York at the request of vaudeville manager, William Hammerstein, is my unfathomable ability to juggle five balls with my feet.

I put my cigar into an ashtray and set down the glass. Twisting the ends of my mustache, I am resolved about what I'm to do next, for I've never been one to pass up an opportunity.

I rise. The ship lurches. Poker chips, chess pieces, and tumblers fall on the floor. With my walking stick, I whack them away and stagger toward the door.

The ship creaks, a slow back and forth. The vessel tilts. I balance myself between the doorway.

The corridor is empty.

I open the door to a first-class suite. What finery, such elegance. There's a diamond stickpin and a ruby ring on the mahogany dresser. Did I mention that I am also a thief? I drop the stickpin and ruby ring into my coat pocket. I open the armoire and glide my hand over the dresses until I choose one.

Cont.

If costumed in one lady's attire, I might draw attention, so I open the door to the next cabin.

"Excuse me, Sir," I say. A man holds a whiskey bottle in one hand and a Bible in the other. "Are you not going on deck?"

"Leave me be young man."

I shut the door.

The next room is charming, even as the furniture slides to the wall, with peacock patterns on overturned chairs, an electric fireplace, a vanity fit for Sarah Bernhardt. Stumbling, I open a chest of drawers grab undergarments and a scarf.

What I need is a warm coat, ladies' boots, and a hat. The lights go off, then on. I must hurry.

I enter a suite across the hall.

The room is in shambles. The dresser is on its side, a chair on its back. I throw the clothes on the bed and go to the trunk and take out a winter coat, lace-up boots, and a hat with a feather.

What I am about to do may seem shameful.

I sit on the edge of the bed next to the heap of clothes and remove my coat, then my tie and collar. My brother, may he rest in peace, comes to mind as I unbutton my shirt.

The binding is tight around my chest, and I begin to unfasten. Charles, was more than a brother, a father, he was (I continue to unwind) to me, a motherless devil-rat, five years to his twelve. The bandage is off. My breasts are revealed.

I remove my trousers and drawers and pull the padding from between my legs. At a young age, Charles dressed me as a boy — "You'll be safer, and we can make a shilling or two." We performed on street corners and in taverns, and as I

Cont.

grew and girls liked me, I liked them back. I am not an impersonator like the popular music hall drags. I am a man, and I've made the best of my oddity.

Naked, I dress.

Perfumes from the clothes make my eyes water. I put my wallet, cuff links, and stolen jewelry into the pocket of the woolen coat and squeeze my feet into the boots.

There is a strangeness to it, and I feel an utter distaste, the way the undergarments rustle and swish. Above the dresser is a mirror. I put on the hat and cover my short hair but leave a fringe that falls over my forehead. The mustache, I peel off and put in my pocket.

Pinching my cheeks, the way I've seen my lovers do, I leave the way I came and go onto the deck.

Such chaos and panic. A man says good-bye to his wife and son as a lifeboat is lowered. Their cries provoke pity.

"Is there room?" I ask in a feminine voice.

"No, Miss," a crew member shouts. "Might be on the other side."

My unease mounts. I hurry among the crowd. My air of detachment collapses as I shove aside men and go around the stern. A lifeboat hangs from the davits.

"Women and children first!"

It's mayhem. Men implore their families to board, promising everything will be all right. From their shabby clothes, it's easy to see they're from steerage.

"What do we have here?" a shipmate yells. He removes a shawl and a scarf from the head of a man trying to board. "Josser."

A woman has the vapors and faints in her husband's arms.

A crowd gathers by a lifeboat hanging from the derricks. Men step aside as I make my way through.

Before me is a woman and her three daughters. Their tattered clothes arouse my sympathy. I slip the ruby ring into the woman's coat pocket.

"Come on, Miss," a deckhand says. He takes my arm and helps me into the boat.

Other than the two in command of rowing, I am the only man.

I dismiss any charge that I am a coward. Be that as it may, it will forever be a blessing, an irony indeed, that what saved me was the hand I was dealt.

Divorced
by
Andrew Senior

At first the ability to exact revenge came as a surprise, but I was determined that she would never be completely free of me. In that I would not stand alone. Everything I had felt since Tamara had divorced me had been compressed into one intense desire: to stand superior over the humiliation. Sometimes it was a bookmark moved a few pages back in the book. Sometimes clothes switched between drawers. Sometimes ornaments shifted between rooms. On one occasion it was a loosened pan handle. Another time, a loosened radiator valve. Nothing too dramatic, I didn't think. Just enough on each visit for a sense of unease and disquiet to culminate. That was the idea.

Habits that lingered showed me when I could act. Bins out a day or so before they needed to be. The front gate firmly closed where usually it swung open across the pavement. The table light in the hall on a timer, 9 to 11pm, when otherwise the house stood in darkness, the rest of the sweeping row of grand Victorian terraces lit up in evening domesticity. The dining room window was my point of entry and exit. It had the original sash which she couldn't afford to replace, easy to open, and close, from the outside.

This time, it was a bottle of bleach from the downstairs loo poured into the big pot plant in the bay window of the lounge. It would create a withered spectacle visible from outside and I liked the idea of that.

Cont.

Through the dining room window came the sound of the wind, catching in the tree that stood on the other side of the garden wall, a sound so familiar, the sound of memory, nights in the golden glow, and the quiet and the stillness, with Tamara.

Once back outside, I stood in the shadows close to the house, making sure I was unobserved. It would be difficult to explain why Alastair Lawrence QC, was creeping around in the undergrowth of his ex-wife's house. I ran across the lawn, intending to leap over the wall on to the path on the other side, and back to where I'd parked the Mercedes.

I had no idea what I'd run into in the dark. Something hard and metal. The clanging sound reverberated through my skull and I remember the sudden shock of the pain, and falling backwards and then nothing.

#

When I came round I was lying on a sofa. My head hurt. I didn't know where I was, although it seemed familiar. There was a man staring at me. The man also looked familiar. He stood silently against the wall.

I heard someone else enter the room, footsteps crossing the carpet.

Tamara knelt down beside me. I held her enthralling gaze, the unique gift of her green eyes. She looked triumphant and beautiful.

Cont.

'Hello Al, nice suit. Remember Ian?'

Ian. From next door. It began to dawn on me what had happened.

'He found you. Well, his dog did. You must have encountered the new pergola. *Every* time I've been away. I knew there was something funny going on.'

None of us spoke. My head was throbbing.

The doorbell rang.

'That was quick.' She turned to Ian and he left the room. Mockingly she stroked my hair. The touch of her hand passed right through me, a flood of warmth and desire, and the fresh realisation of what was dead and gone. She leant close and whispered, 'I never imagined you'd be capable of something like this, Al.'

Ian walked back into the room, a sneer on his face. I managed to prop myself up to see the two people who were following him. Then with a slow exhale of breath, I laid back on the sofa and closed my eyes.

'Alastair Lawrence?' asked one of the policemen.

Memoir

Dance Republic
by
Chiara Vascotto

This should all be familiar, but I am gripped by alienation.

I have been here before, but not like this. I have done this before, but not like this. I am not who I was.

A chasm separates the last time I danced, just over one year ago, and today. I have survived lockdown, divorce, loss of income and a house move, but the prospect of this one lesson feels daunting, unsurmountable.

Underneath my old dance clothes, there is a new skin itching and making it impossible to settle. My favourite grey leggings and the matching top no longer fit. It is not just the Covid kilos, the slight roundness that week after week of stillness and uncertainty set up shop around my hips. I had assumed divorce would mean a simple equation of 'life-as-I-know-it minus husband', and I was ok with the prospect. Enticed, even. But no sooner had I pulled the lever and instructed my lawyer, than everything I had taken for granted began to collapse, like the house of cards it was. Friendships, lifestyle, preferences, it all fell away as I watched, bewildered. It rarely felt disastrous. More often than not, it felt necessary, and strangely interesting. But what would emerge from the rubble remained elusive.

I have danced before, but not like this. I have danced with Ed before, but not like this. Ed, the Latin dance wizard who ran my weekly classes before the world transformed beyond recognition. Does he still exist, IRL? I had seen his digital image, and that of his other class regulars, on zoom tiles. Everyone jaded, everyone trying to stay sane. I had attempted to jig to his online classes, despite the sound lag, despite the lure of the fridge, of the cats, of Instagram. These efforts had only amplified the longing. And now? Does his dance fire still burn bright? More importantly, does mine?

Cont.

I remember the first time I tried the class, in what feels like a previous life. When face masks were the stuff of movies, and where I was still in my "for better, for worse" contract. On the surface, I was curious about trying these Latin styles without the need for a partner. In truth, I wanted one more hour away from home and from its quiet desperation. I perched on the studio's staircase, as a stream of clickety clackety tap dancers cleared the room. My desire to delay the reyurn to reality only marginally stronger than my apprehension around the new challenge ahead.

It was his shoes I saw first. Red high-top trainers, paired with black track pants and a black vest. An urban dancer, not the orange ponytailed sleazebag I had feared. Despite his imposing figure, he beamed a sunny smile as he took his place in front row, to the notes of Camilla Cabello.

My eyes never left his red shoes, as I tried to pick up the footwork. They tickled the floor with tantalising agility. They were going, going, flying, pinging to the rhythm with joyful precision. Dorothy shoes, down an undiscovered yellow brick road. Sunny Cuban vibes transformed the dreary evening into an hour of blissful release. His choreography was challenging yet intuitive, and I could not hide the elation as the combinations eased into my body. We swayed from sassy salsa to cheeky cha chas, from jumpy jives to balmy bachatas. I lapped it all up.

It was the first time I felt I could access this particular dance world, a realm that had called and frightened me in equal measures. I had looked at it from the outskirts, never daring to have a go. There were the nights at Floridita, London's Cuban club, where Carlos Acosta would rock up, oozing star quality and pheromones, and dance with impossibly beautiful women in miniature dresses. There were the times I craned my neck to catch the sensual moves at Pineapple studios, on my way to yet another hour of ballet discipline. Partner dancing was seductive, intoxicating, as well as fraught and unattainable.

Cont.

But Ed's classes were a way in. My practice gained momentum, and in an impulsive bout I plucked up the courage to sign up for a weekend intensive to learn to move with a partner. I was counting the days with dread and anticipation.

And then the world grinding to a halt. The intolerable becoming impossible to ignore. Twelve years of marriage unravelling.

"There she is!" I see his smile, his arms wide open, drawing me into the first of many hugs. "So glad you decided to dance with me! I thought you'd never ask!" His blend of warmth and delicate scents greet me. I glance down. On his feet, the Dorothy shoes, ready for magic.

***

The studio is small and bare, but welcoming. Two large windows flood the space with natural daylight even in this bleak midwinter day. A tall plant, the room's sole dweller, stands in a corner. As I step in, I hear my fears ramping up in my head. I am not a dancer I am not a dancer I am not a dancer, they say.

But Ed has other ideas and has already switched on the music. We walk to the beat. It is like walking, he tells me. I am reminded of my first ballet teacher, and of how this used to be one of her favourite sayings. I soften a little.

"And then we can go sideways…" his hand reaches mine and tugs me to the left. The contact makes me jolt. I am reminded that this dance involves touch. Of course, it does. What was I *thinking*! I feel intensely unprepared. And yet my body relaxes. He takes my other hand, and to my relief, I notice how pleasantly dry his skin is. I remember watching him as he guided us through the Latin Burn class. He would be so drenched that sometimes he would discretely change his top halfway through the lesson, much to our

Cont.

furtive excitement. I, like others, would busy myself with my shoelaces, or my water bottle, whilst allowing my eyes to wander back to his bare chest. Enticing as the sight was, the prospect of holding a damp hand was very off-putting, and for a long time enough of a deterrent to make me forget all about salsa. "Or backwards..." Ed continues and explains the type of contact that dance partners need, to speak without words. It is a level of pressure detectable enough to make your presence and willingness felt, but not too much as to feel tense or dominating. Alert, yet malleable. Two forces coming together, as equal. I find the idea intensely beautiful.

I am throwing all my concentration at the dance, and I seem to be assisted by beginner's luck. The footwork comes easily. The steps are the same as the ones we danced to in our group class. But I am about to experience the one variable that makes all the difference. The hold. There are no rows of dancers between us, no mirrors to mediate our interaction. It is us, in a new proximity. "And this is how it goes..." A *whoosh* of senses envelops me as his arm effortlessly finds its way around me. His body warmth, the smooth cotton of his T-shirt, the gentle hints of cologne, deodorant, fabric conditioner, toothpaste... It smells like a safe place. I feel his body, solid and muscular but with the slightest layer of flesh, suggesting he is a lover of life, more than of gyms and steroids. It's all ok. It's all more than ok.

I am having to adjust to this surprisingly welcome closeness, whilst keeping up with the movements and the counts. I swing between comfort and unease. We change directions and I am thrown by the new landmarks. I skip a beat, I stumble, but I have his frame to come back to.

In an attempt to feel in control of the dance (rookie mistake, I will come to learn), I rush, and the timing goes awry. "You have more time than you think," he smiles. "It's one, two, three...and a *pause*.

Cont.

Five, six, seven, and another *pause*." I count and I make the pause happen. My hips begin to sway, my steps to find their ease. It all begins to feel like a story, a feeling, not just a string of movements.

One, two, three. *Pause.* Five, six, seven. *Pause.* O. M. G. *Pause.* This. Is. Great. *Pause.*

I must be doing something right because Ed's face has lit up. I see the same glint I found in his mirrored image in the group class, if we all landed on the right spot, to the beat. A teacher's joy. I keep stepping, I keep counting, I keep tuning into our contact to gauge the next step. I feel like I have cracked a secret code. It's exhilarating.

"Let's step it up" he squeals, his Dorothy shoes fizzing as he finds a new track on his phone. Of course, he would want to step it up. Like any gifted teacher, he is both accepting and demanding. He would often ramp up the tempo in our classes, finishing with the fastest, bounciest of Jives to the notes of *You Can't Stop the Beat*, the whole five minutes, and forty-four seconds of it, leaving us euphoric, spent, yet wildly alive. This time, the ebullient sound of *A Vida Es Um Carnaval* ripples across the walls. It is a much faster salsa, but I can keep up, grinning, incredulous. We high five, ecstatic. Surely, that's the way to call it a day. Ed hesitates, then he blurts out: "one more thing, just let me teach you this one more thing!" "Ed, there's no need to teach me everything in one day! I *am* coming back, you know?" I hear myself say. And I know this to be true. This is only the beginning. "Just have a go," he insists, demonstrating the move. I do. He beams. "I *knew* it! A first for me! I have taught you all the basic moves in one day!" He is genuinely chuffed, as he shakes his head. He bear-hugs me. "You are *amazing*."

Am I amazing, I wonder in the changing room, as I peel off my leggings, the salsa rhythm still pulsating in my ears. Am I amazing? I leave the studio with what I think is a shimmy, my parka unzipped, oblivious to the January wind.

***

Cont.

Once home, I realise that elation has morphed into discomfort. I am edgy, pinging from room to room, tackling tasks only to abandon them moments later. Why this unrest? Do I miss my daughter? Since the separation, Mondays are always ambivalent, with life for two returning to solo living, the flat tidier but emptier, the silence at once welcome and uncomfortable. But no. Zoe and I have found our way to be with each other, our new rhythm, for when we are together and when we are apart. It must be something else.

Picking at some cheese and tomatoes, with yet another episode of Friends as my dinner companion, I get teary at the Ross and Rachel drama. I switch the TV off, sling the plate into the dishwasher but it drops and breaks. I brush up its shattered remains, vexed. Maybe a shower will do it. I allow the hot water to rain down on me and pour a generous helping of lavender oil on my hand, breathing in the scent.

"Hey, lady!"

And I remember. I bolt out of the shower, scoop myself up in the bath sheet and curl up on the bed, hugging myself. Three weeks ago, my first Boxing Day on my own. I had taken myself out to the high street, to escape my empty flat. A smattering of shops were open, spitting out tinsel and tat that was already devoid of lustre.

A cashpoint. I might as well. My single life involves foreseeing, planning, being prepared. Cash is always useful. The machine was blinking and bleating. *Please take your card. Please take your card*, it repeated, its orifices empty. Maybe I should leave it. Maybe this machine is dodgy. *Ping. Please insert your card.* Here we go. Somehow, as I absentmindedly punched in my PIN, I got a fleeting thought about my Brazilian friends never daring to use a hole in the wall on the street. Too dangerous, they say.

Please take your card. I did. *Please take your cash promptly.* I did this, too.

Cont.

"Hey, lady!" I saw his eyes, dark and unsettling. They made me want to recoil. "I was using this machine," he said, "and it did not give out the twenty pounds I requested." I felt my body chemistry altering, almost tasting the adrenaline spike.

"You have my twenty pounds" he said, drawing into my space, crossing the invisible line between anonymity and danger. In my cold hands, the cash, the card, the wallet. The handbag unzipped across my body. I fought the urge to freeze. Why does it get ugly so quickly?

"One moment, please." My heart was pumping. My trembling hands hastily stuffed it all into my handbag. I stepped back. He stepped closer. "There was no cash being dispensed when I started to use the machine," I said. I knew it was true. And I knew it wouldn't matter because he was edging closer. Would he rob me, or hit me? Or both?

"I have just withdrawn my own cash, sorry," I continued, "If there's been a problem, the bank can fix it, you should speak to them." I started to walk away. There were people about but what my mind saw was the same deserted road where I was assaulted two decades ago. All that existed was that same ominous dread. I will never make it home.

"You have my twenty pounds!" he yelled, close at my heels, as I took faster, bigger strides away from him. "Hey, lady!" and then, louder: "I am calling the police!" My eyes darted around and I spottted an open convenience store. It became my sole route to safety.

"Don't you walk off with my money, lady!"

I called to the first shop assistant I saw. He must have been in his late teens. He was scrawny, bored. He did not want to be there, nor did he look like he could handle what was to come. "Excuse me…" I approached him. He saw the man who had followed me and looked more scared than I was.

Cont.

"She has my money!" the man continued.

"Just let me check already!" I welcomed the unfamiliar resolve in my voice, and the hand gesture that said back off. Maybe I wouldn't have to take his BS, in this safer space.

"She has my money!" he repeated to the dazed shoppers scouring tired-looking gift sets.

"I may well have your money" I said, trying to stay calm. "I simply want to check. I know how much I have withdrawn. If there is more than that in my handbag, then that is your money, and I will certainly give it to you."

I will never know what truly happened next.

In the depths of my handbag, I saw the freshly pressed notes, still at large. I could have sworn my eyes counted six of them. Six twenty-pound bills. I knew I had withdrawn one hundred pounds. Relief laced with embarrassment mounted within me. "My bad," I said conciliatorily. Maybe this was, after all, a genuine misunderstanding. "I did get your twenty, here," I took one of the notes to give it to him. "I would not hassle you like that otherwise," he said earnestly, black eyes fixed on me, swiping the note before I could fully hand it to him. "Merry Christmas", he said, walking off. "Merry Christmas," I replied with a strained smile. I felt the shoppers settling back to the sales. People had noticed our exchange. Perhaps someone had been poised to intervene. Perhaps. Nobody had said a word.

I did not need any toiletries, but I was not ready to face the street again just yet, so I meandered down the pungent deodorant aisle, then through the hair dyes display, waiting for my heart rate to subside. I roamed the vitamins section, trying to ignore Wham's *Last Christmas* in the airwaves, as well as an unnamed, sinking feeling. I scanned brightly coloured shower gel bottles, dismissing their promise of smoother skin and I knew I had to check my handbag again.

Cont.

The bills were there where I had left them. Only there were just four of them. I looked again. Just four. Did I really have six notes to begin with? Or did my survival instinct, my past trauma rustle up an optical illusion to allow me to fob the guy off? Was he a hypnotist? A con man?

"A dickhead" concluded my friend Martha matter-of-factly, over mulled wine, two days later. "London, innit?" added Alice shrugging her shoulders. "Full of nutters." Then both, in unison: "you did the right thing."

"He could have followed you home, had he not got the money."

"What's twenty quid, in the scheme of things?"

What's twenty quid, I think right now, pressing my towel on my damp, cold legs. What's twenty quid, but another female tax, another price tag for the illusion of safety. The cabs home, the therapy sessions, now this. Invoices that keep claiming their remittance, twenty years on.

A tear plops onto the towel and I realise I am sobbing. But it is not fear, or sadness. It feels like relief. Because although that…incident (I do not know what to call it…perhaps the invasion, the extortion, the episode of everyday violence?) Because although that happened, I was ultimately safe. Not just in the outcome, but in its unfolding. I did not freeze nor lose my voice. I had regained some control and brought myself to safety.

I still feel the violation, amongst other things, of my personal space. But I am also, suddenly, defiantly aware of how safe I had felt, a few hours ago, locking arms with Ed.

That Ed's proximity felt welcome and inviting, now feels like a triumph. That I could experience this so soon after the accident, now feels like a miracle. My sense of trust may be dented, but it is not beyond repair.

I dry my hands. I dry my eyes with the back of my wrist and feel my cat Samba headbutting me gently, rubbing his face round my ankles. There, there, goes his gentle purr.

Cont.

My phone beeps and see that Ed has texted me. "You did great today. Well done, Queen of Salsa!"

I did do great today. And in the past two years, as I got myself back to safety, back to life. And in the past two decades, surviving and repurposing violence.

"I loved it, Ed!" I text back. "When is your next free slot?"

A grinning emoji pings on my screen. "10am tomorrow. You game?" I choose the sunshades emoji: "You betcha!"

***

I have been here before, but not like this. I am not who I was. The place, too, is not what it was. Its former name is now replaced by a simple door number. Seven.

But I remember it being called Evolve, and it being a longed-for destination. It was a place of muted hope during my darker years of marriage, its name a promise as compelling as it was elusive, whilst I tried in vain to get unstuck. Evolve used to host personal development seminars on positive thinking and 'the art of manifesting'. I flocked to them, hungry for change, furious at my inability to bring it about.

I wanted to embrace the cheerful optimism of the facilitators, and the possibility that I could think my way out of my own disasters. I duly compiled reams of gratitude lists, as my personal life continued to implode. I wrote alone, my cat as my sole witness, sitting quietly next to me. I did not feel especially grateful. Of course, there was always something to be thankful for. And yet, and yet. The unnamed truth refused to be ignored. I cannot *be,* I thought, I cannot *live* in this marriage. I may die, if things do not change.

Cont.

In these seminars, I made myself imagine another existence, and stubbornly wrote about how I might be living instead. Glimmers of new beginnings did manifest, but they were always fleeting and precarious, vanishing at the stroke of midnight. Job opportunities came and went, bait in which I'd get caught and badly hurt. The possibility of other men appeared then disappeared, like taunting holograms. The years ticked by. I would kiss my daughter goodnight, tuck her in her pink bed, plush bunny in tow. She was so little and precious and my mind would scream "I can't, I won't." I had resigned to feeling alien in my own home, my space shared unwisely and unwillingly, my sense of safety eroding daily.

Years on, what used to be Evolve now stands in its new incognito guise and freshly revarnished window. It looks the part, down these South Kensington mews, wedged in between a pooch day spa and an antique car dealership. SW3 staples. It is now a hideaway for those in the know, with time and cash to spare. I am no longer one of them.

Is this Square One again? For so long my life had felt like Groundhog Day, I am terrified of finding myself in the same funk.

I have read somewhere that the way we learn is not so much of a curve, but a set of spirals, only apparently returning to the same spot, revisiting it instead from new depths and new perspectives, as our growth deepens. Maybe, then, more than Snakes and Ladders, this is a game of Monopoly. I am here again, but with new assets. Perhaps less wealthy, but somehow richer. I have passed go again and got my twenty pounds. Twenty pounds. A chill down my spine. *"Hey, lady!"* For an instant I freeze. Then I let out a big breath, which condenses in the cold air and I push the studio door.

Cont.

"It's the Queen of Salsa!" Ed beams as he greats me. I lower my gaze and I feel my neck burning, as I scurry to the changing rooms.

Our impending proximity calls and scares me. I fold and unfold my clothes, unsure of what to do with them. I cannot decide between the two leggings I brought, both black and anonymous, and I want to run a mile.

"Shall we?" I hear his cheerful invitation from the other room.

We are back in hold, and I want to feel good about it. My body does, but my mind is erratic. Ed's shape, smells and warmth are becoming a little more familiar, yet for a while I cannot settle. I stumble and freeze, lose count, trip up.

I don't dare to look at him but when I do, he looks unphased by my tentative moves. He is patient, attentive, precise in his feedback. "Too many steps," or: "shift the weight onto the right leg." Simple instructions that do not spell doom, or failure, and that get me back on track. "Don't worry," he adds "it just needs to get in the body." I breathe. I count. I keep going.

Vente Negra plays on. It is a slow but groovy salsa, and my concentration eventually lands on the one, two, three, *pause,* five, six, seven, *pause.* Our movements return to harmony, my body softens, my breathing eases.

I begin to discover Ed's many codes to impart instructions intuitively, non-verbally. The wiggling of his fingers when I have forgotten to give him my hand, the gentle tugging to adjust our direction of travel, his way of finding my eyes when they fix on his Dorothy shoes, and of bringing them back up to his face, helping my posture unfurl to a more confident stance. As my gaze settles on his, and I let the music sway me, I learn that:

Cont.

His eyes are not brown but forest green.

There's a warm, almost auburn kick to his beard.

He smells of Dolce and Gabbana's Light Blue, only better. Dancing begins to feel like home again.

"Well done! So good!" Ed is hugging me, and I realise that our hour together has passed. I return his embrace more easily this time.

"Let's book next week!" I say, whipping out my phone. He raises his eyebrows in mock surprise, as if to say: 'get you!' He looks genuinely happy. "I have a regular free slot, actually…" he says. I hold my breath. It feels so lavish to do this. He smiles: "no pressure. Just think about it."

I leave the studio, parka draped round my arm, sashaying out of the mews and into the London chaos. I dribble the swarm of tourists directed to the V&A and hop on the bus. I get to the top deck and settle on the front seat, the expanse of the Science Museum before me. As route 430 chugs on, I mull over the last hour. My hands still smell of Light Blue, and my mind still thinks of the regular slot.

Ed's lessons are worth every penny and are not unreasonably priced. But they still feel extravagant, at a time when I need to curb my spending.

The divorce negotiations had revealed just how foggy my financial awareness had been. Money, a lot of it, came and went. How could I fritter it away, just to stave off boredom and frustration? Handbags I did not even like. Prim and proper dresses I never wore. Nothing to show for.

My lawyer had forensically analysed my accounts, through ominous graphs and charts. She kept telling me to *have a ten-year plan*, at a time when I hardly knew my own name.

Cont.

To appease her, I did come up with The Plan. I would grow my client base, hike up my fees, and hey presto, return to badass consultant status. I was that, one lifetime ago. I can be that again. My lawyer merrily proceeded to input the new figures I had plucked up from thin air. The dreaded graphs went from red to green, the charts inverted their course, from calamitous descent to glorious success. It looked like a Plan.

Only, my soul wanted none of it. The theoretical picture of stability, of financial safety looked alien, dangerous even. I had left that life, and it had felt like a lucky escape.

I was not who I used to be, nor did I want to go back.

I still do not know who I am becoming, but I do know that dance is where I begin again.

The bus is approaching leafy Fulham, where I need to get off. I will find the money. On its app, I gleefully cancel my membership to The World's Most Depressing Gym. The monthly fee hardly covers for one of my salsa lessons, but it's a start. Maybe I can leverage my consultancy skills without becoming the she-wolf of Wall Street. Maybe I can rise my fees a little. Or a lot.

Before I hop off, I book Ed's regular slot.

My soul wants to dance. And I'll let it.

Fiction

Works of prose in which imaginary stories either realistic or unrealistic are told.

JOURNEY ACROSS DARTMOOR
by
Andy Stewart

Two slim middle-aged women, dressed in jeans, T-shirts and cycle helmets, were outside the village stores. They heaved the laden rucksacks onto their backs.

"What's up, Martha McIntosh? You look worried."

"Is it that obvious?"

"Only to me. You forget I've known you a very long time."

"It's my Anthony visit tomorrow. I dread the journey on that bloody bus."

"Suppose I come with you? Not when you go into the room. I wouldn't want to intrude. But I could bring my sketch pad. I haven't done a picture of the moors for ages."

"That would be so kind of you, Tess. Are you sure you don't mind?"

"To be honest it would be good to get out onto Dartmoor again. It's one of my most favourite places and I prefer wide open spaces to being cooped up." Like synchronised swimmers at an unspoken command, they each swung a leg over their bicycles and sat astride the saddles. "I'm assuming that Graham hasn't offered to take you tomorrow?"

"Everyone copes with things in their own way."

They pedalled off in opposite directions to their homes.

*

Cont.

The following day the sunlit countryside was sliding past their bus window. There was rolling moorland as far as the eye could see, with little dots of grazing sheep and ponies scattered around the ancient landscape like pepper grounds. Martha's eyes were in idle mode. She wasn't taking anything in. Her thoughts were lost, nestling at her destination and her son. She felt a hand on her arm.

"You okay?"

"Most of these are regulars on this trip," Martha said quietly by way of reply, looking round the half-filled bus. "Some of them tried to strike up a conversation with me in the beginning, in an effort to share the experience. I daresay they meant well, but I know all about how it feels, thank you very much."

The man in the seat in front of them was wiggling his index finger in his right ear. He had started doing this gently, but the process was becoming more vigorous by the second. He was moving it so fast that his hand had become blurred.

Martha tapped him on his shoulder. "Are you alright?"

He turned round, digit half-way in, the frantic jiggling temporarily ceasing. Martha estimated he was in his early thirties. She was seldom wrong about ages. He was tanned and of athletic build.

"There's something in my ear."

"Yeah. It's your bloody finger, mate!" shouted a man overflowing the seat behind Martha. He had one leg sticking out into the aisle. He was unable to place his thighs together due to their girth. His face was a deep crimson, his large ears sticking out like pancakes at right-angles to his head.

Cont.

"It's buzzing. I think there's an insect in there," said the finger-in-the-ear man, his voice rising.

"Must be an earwig." This suggestion came from a young woman sitting on the other side of the gangway to Martha and Tess. The corpulent bloke guffawed, causing his double chins to wobble. Blobs of red jam, the colour of his suffuse cheeks, escaped from the large doughnut he was enjoying, sliding from one corner of his mouth onto the collar of his open-necked shirt.

"Earwigs can burrow in to your brain to lay their eggs." It was the young woman again. She was wearing a bobble hat and a scarf that looked like it had been knitted in a hurry. Ginger curls poked out from under her hat and the freckles scattered across her nose and cheeks looked like they had been applied with a spray gun.

The large man behind Martha started to laugh. It was a deep bass note that reverberated around the bus, as though he was an opera singer warming up before a performance. In an instant his chuckle turned into audible choking. Martha and Tess swung round in their seats. He wheezed and panted, his hands grasping at empty air, his eyes wide open in distress.

"He's gone blue," said Tess.

Martha stood and moved behind the chubby choker. By now all the passengers were watching, fixed to their seats by the glue of morbid fascination. The driver was oblivious to the drama unfolding behind him on his number ninety-eight bus.

Cont.

"Help me stand him up," Martha said to Tess, her voice calm.

A man, with the tattooed words 'love' and 'hate' spelt out over his knuckles, got up from his seat and offered to help. His hair looked like it had been cut with a hedge trimmer, leaving him with a scalp of short bristles resembling a badly worn toothbrush. Under Martha's instruction the three of them hauled the choking man to his feet, and manipulated him into being bent double at the waist over the back of his seat. He was producing some interesting squeaks and whistles.

"He's too obese for the Heimlich manoeuvre," Martha announced.

There was absolute silence as Martha delivered five hefty blows between his shoulder blades with the heel of her hand, with as much force as she could muster. To her relief a large fragment of trapped doughnut became dislodged and shot out of his mouth like a cork out of a champagne bottle, landing on the floor of the bus.

The passengers applauded. The beneficiary of Martha's skills straightened up and, grabbing the back of the seat in front of him, inhaled noisily long and hard before giving a sighing breath out. He wiped the sweat from his forehead, walked forward a couple of paces and sat down heavily in his original seat. "Where's my doughnut? It cost me two pounds fifty."

"Ungrateful sod," observed tattooed knuckles.

Tess looked down. It was crushed under her foot. She raised her shoe.

A sweet little girl with pigtails and a Mickey Mouse T-shirt scuttled over and peeled the delicacy off the floor of the bus, before handing it to the doughnut's owner. He studied the squashed doughy mess for a moment, gave it a wipe with his sleeve and popped it into his mouth.

Cont.

"Some people are unbelievable!" said Tess as they returned to their seats. "Are you always that calm?"

"Not always. But being the senior nurse in a busy casualty department helps."

With a squeal of brakes, the bus came to an abrupt halt. Some small items of luggage fell out of the racks above their heads into the aisle.

"Why are we stopping here, in the middle of the moor?" asked the man with the tattooed knuckles. "Don't tell me we've run out of petrol."

"I won't tell you we've run out of petrol," said the driver in his broad Devon accent, "for two very good reasons. Firstly, this is a diesel vehicle. And secondly, the fuel gauge is showing the tank to be three quarter's full, and I've never known it to be wrong yet."

"So why…?" knuckles persisted.

"If you look out of the window you'll see why," said the driver.

They looked, as instructed.

"Sheep," said the sweet little girl, pointing excitedly through the window.

"Well, they aren't camels, that's for sure," agreed the driver. "They've decided to sit down across the middle of our route. I'll need some volunteers to help me shift them."

"Do they bite?" enquired the little girl's mother.

"No, but I do" came the reply.

Cont.

Martha, Tess and most of the other passengers helped the driver to shoo the animals back onto the grass verges on either side of the moorland road. It took them ten minutes as several of the creatures, having been moved, then decided to return to the exact spot where they had been only moments before. After ten minutes the sheep became bored and wandered off.

When Martha and Tess climbed back onto the bus the man sitting in the seat in front of them still had his finger in his ear.

"The buzzing's stopped" he informed Martha as she walked by.

"You can take your finger out then."

"No, I can't." He looked at her defiantly.

"Why not?"

"Because it's stuck. That's why not."

"I'm a nurse. Let me see if I can help."

In spite of Martha's best efforts, accompanied by much pulling and wiggling, the finger remained firmly in place.

"Has anyone got any liquid with them?" she asked her fellow travellers. "Preferably something oily."

The woman with the freckles piped up. "I've got some Oil of Olay in my handbag. Will that do?"

"Let's give it a go." Freckles left her seat and walked up towards Martha in the middle of the bus, handing over a small bottle.

Martha turned to the man with the finger stuck in his ear. "What's your name?"

Cont.

"Maurice."

"Maurice, I'm Martha. I want you to tilt your head to one side so your ear with the finger in it is uppermost."

"Like this?"

"That's good. Now I'm going to trickle a little of this pink fluid into your ear. It may feel a bit cold." She tipped the bottle so some of the contents ran into his ear alongside the wedged finger.

"Keep absolutely still. We're going to wait a couple of minutes. The oil should act as a lubricant." Martha looked up. Everyone had left their seats and were crowding around her.

"Sit down, you lot!" yelled the driver over his shoulder. "No standing allowed. It's against the company's safety regulations."

They all ignored him. Martha seized Maurice's right hand and moved it around for a moment before giving it a sharp tug. Out came his finger with a slurping sound.

"Thank you," said Maurice, his facial muscles crumpling with relief.

Everyone returned to their seats, the excitement over.

"It's odd your finger got stuck, Maurice. Do you mind if I examine your ear?"

"Be my guest, but for God's sake don't get *your* finger stuck in there!"

"Don't worry, I've done this before." Martha slowly inserted her little finger into the man's ear canal. After a few seconds she

Cont.

withdrew it.

"Are you a surfer?"

"How on earth did you know that?"

Martha laughed. "I felt a bony lump sticking out into your ear canal. That's why your finger got stuck. The lump is called an exostosis." Maurice raised his eyebrows in alarm. "It's nothing sinister. It's a bone growth caused by exposure to cold water, most commonly seen in surfers. If it's causing you any problems, you can have the lump removed."

"I have been getting a bit hard of hearing lately. I'll go and see my GP. Should I stop surfing in the meantime? It will be one heck of a wait until I can get an appointment at the surgery."

"Why not get yourself some earplugs from the chemist to use when you surf, until you get to see your doctor.?"

"Brilliant. I'll do that."

"It was lucky you were on this bus today," said Tess. "I dread to think what would have happened otherwise."

"We're here," said Martha. They disembarked along with half-a-dozen of the other passengers, and stood together looking at an imposing arch built with large blocks of alternating pink and brown granite. In the middle of the arch above their heads was an inscription in Latin.

"Parcere Subjectis. It means Spare the Vanquished." Martha spoke in a weary monotone. "This place was used to house prisoners from the Napoleonic Wars. Nowadays it's a Category C prison."
"Category C?"

Cont.

"It's used for non-violent white-collar offenders." Martha stared grimly up at the arch. "I don't see why they couldn't have given Anthony a non-custodial sentence. Embezzlement from a wealthy bank is a victimless crime if you ask me. And it was his first offence."

"How long will you be?" Tess asked Martha, a wobble in her voice.

"An hour. Why not meet me back here in sixty minutes? It's a nice day for a walk on the moors. No rain to spoil your sketchpad."

"I presume they're expecting you?"

"Oh yes. No spontaneous visits are allowed. I have to book over the phone and wait for an email confirming I can come. They always ask for my date of birth. God only knows why."

"Anthony was lucky to have a Mum like you."

Martha swallowed hard. "He used to be allowed two one hour visits every four weeks. Kurt and myself alternating; his boyfriend and his mother. His sexuality is another reason he and his father fell out. I used to worry about Anthony being picked on because he was gay. You read such dreadful things, especially about what happens in prisons. Perhaps white-collar criminals are a cut above your usual villains, more civilised in their treatment of their fellow man. At least they didn't bang him up with a bunch of murderers."

Tess went very pale.

"Are you okay, Tess? You look awful."

"It's my fear of confined spaces. I get this overwhelming urge to break into a run and get as far away as possible. I'm just being daft. A bit of moorland air will "You're not being daft at all. Are you still having counselling for your claustrophobia?"

Cont.

"It wasn't making much difference. And we were starting to go over the same old stuff. I've jacked it in for the moment."

"I really appreciate your coming with me today. You'll never know how much it helps, having you here." Martha rummaged through her bag. Her hand emerged clutching a packet of Nuttall's Mintoes. "Take these to suck as you sketch. I look forward to seeing what you draw."

Tess headed off in the direction of the nearest tor. With her artist's bag over her shoulder, she paused for a moment to gaze back at the prison's silhouette. Martha waved before turning to go under the arch.

She entered the small familiar visiting room, situated beside the larger communal area where the other visitors met with their imprisoned loved ones. Brick walls painted an institutional pale green. A solitary window with bars resembling a noughts and crosses game, a beam of sunlight landing on the edge of the table. That and the two chairs were the only furniture.

Anthony always looked wan and vulnerable sitting at that table, Martha perched opposite him. She wanted to have him back home and feed him up. All the other visitors had a warden lurking in the background, just in case somebody kicked off. For Martha it was different. She was afforded privacy. Terry saw to that.

"You must be counting the days to your release, Anthony. How has the new job been going? I'm guessing you've really enjoyed working in the prison gardens. All that lovely fresh air."

Cont.

There was no reply. It was a one-sided conversation. Her love hurt, the way love often can. She wanted to hug him, so very much. But that was impossible. She could sense him. He was everywhere in this awful place.

"Time's up, Martha." The precious allocated minutes had ebbed away, a kindly voice breaking into her desert of sadness.

A gentle hand rested on her shoulder. She placed one of her own hands over it. "Thank you, Terry." She knew Terry understood. She would always be grateful that it had been Terry who had found Anthony dangling in his cell on that dreadful day, exactly five years ago; Terry who had cut him down and cradled him.

"Shall we see you next July the fifth, Martha?"

She nodded. "And every July the fifth, for as long as I live."

THE OLD LADIES BENCH
by
Jeane Ende

When Golda Rosen's middle son married Leah Schwartz' eldest daughter the two women became *machitanisters*, a Yiddish word that refers to the bond between the mothers of a husband and a wife. Jewish women sometimes use the word in place of a given name, affectionately saying, "hello *machitanister*," when they greet each other.

However, Leah and Golda weren't fond of each other and saw no reason to pretend they were. They were always polite to each other, and believed that was all that should be expected of them. The two women had known each other for more than 20 years and lived three blocks apart but always used surnames when they met.

"Good day, Mrs. Rosen," Leah said when they met.

"Good day, Mrs. Schwartz," Golda would answer.

One bright October day in 1955, right after lunch, Golda slipped her gnarled feet into her worn, leather slippers, glanced at the candle burning in a small glass next to the kitchen sink and shuffled out the door of her ground-floor apartment. She slowly made her way to the long, grey wooden bench in the alley between the house where she lived in an apartment below her oldest son and his family, and the identical two-family house where her youngest son and his family lived.

A few years ago, when she started having trouble walking, her sons had the bench made so she could sit outside and get some air. It had a high back because she sometimes had trouble with her spine, and a wide slat near the ground where a short woman like Golda could rest her feet The bench had recently been repainted after she pointed out the stains made by bird droppings. Today it was warm from the afternoon sun and Golda sighed contentedly as she sat down.

Cont.

She took a piece of rock candy out of her pocket and sucked on it as she chatted with passing neighbors, finding out what was happening in everyone's life. When no one was around she quietly chanted to herself, a tune hummed so softly it could barely be heard over the passing traffic. From her seat Golda could see all the way down Astor Avenue, the main thoroughfare in her three block kingdom in the Bronx, and she watched Leah Schwartz briskly head toward her, clutching a large brown purse that matched her sturdy walking shoes and a bulky shopping bag.

I wonder if she'll fit me into her busy schedule today, thought Golda. Maybe she has a new praise-worthy activity and she wants to make sure I know about it.

"Hello. It's nice to see you Mrs. Schwartz," said Golda when the other woman was a few feet away. "Would you like to sit down on my bench?"

"It's nice to see you Mrs. Rosen. I think I will join you for just a minute," said Leah carefully putting her shopping bag, which contained a pound of only slightly bruised tomatoes and a few other vegetables, at the end of the bench.

Leah had asked her daughter to get the tomatoes for her from the Italian market on Eastchester Road, explaining that they were having a sale. Her daughter insisted it wasn't worth making a special trip, there were plenty of tomatoes in the refrigerator.

"Those tomatoes are too expensive to use for stewing," said Leah. "If you're too tired I'll go myself." Her daughter shrugged and walked away. Since it was a nice day Leah decided to walk to the market and save the bus fare but now, although she tried not to show it, she was tired and her bunions were hurting.

Cont.

As she sat down Leah wondered, as usual, why Golda didn't get some pillows to put on the hard bench. Even though she was well-padded, Leah knew that her bottom would soon begin to ache. She was sure Golda, who had considerably less padding, must be uncomfortable too. But Leah never suggested that Golda get them some cushions from her apartment and Golda never offered.

"So Mrs. Schwartz, what have you been doing lately?" Golda asked.

"Well, since you ask, I made a cake for my friend Lester yesterday," said Leah. "He lives by himself and does his own cooking. He mentioned he'd been to the bakery so I decided to make something for him so he doesn't waste his money.

"I use only one egg, half a stick of butter and just a little milk and sugar," she said. "My cakes are always delicious, I just have the knack. And if I do say so myself, I know how to get the most from my money."

Golda raised her eyebrows and pursed her lips. "Couldn't have been much of a cake," she said. "I did some baking yesterday too, and when I make a cake I use a dozen eggs, a pound of butter, a gallon of milk and lots of sugar. I never think about how much I'm spending. Good food is worth whatever it costs."

Leah shook her head and the women sat quietly. They watched a group of teenagers stroll by, a large radio that played loud music perched on the shoulder of the tallest one.

Unlike Golda, Leah didn't have her own apartment. She lived with her daughter and son-in-law, a few blocks away, in the back bedroom of a brick two-family house similar to the ones owned by Golda's other sons. Most people in the neighborhood had aged relatives living in their down-stairs apartments--in-laws, maiden aunts, or cousins. Her daughter and son-in-law had expected Leah to do the same. However Leah insisted she didn't need her own apartment and was happier seeing the place produce rent.

"I'm out all day, why do I need to take care of an apartment?" she told people who inquired about the arrangement. "This way I can easily babysit and help Helen with her housework."

Every Monday Leah made large pots of stew from the

Cont.

cheapest cuts of meat, special delicacies like calf's foot jelly, a green aspic with shiny globs of fat that her grandchildren dared each other to taste, and desserts made from marked down bruised fruits. She ate the same meal every day until it was all finished.

"If it's good today it'll be even better tomorrow," she said.

Leah frequently offered to cook for the whole family, eager to showcase her hard-won knowledge of how to scrimp and save, but Helen always vetoed this idea. She was proud that her husband made a good living, that her family didn't have to worry about the cost of food and they had luxuries like the fancy dishwasher that Leah refused to use saying it was for lazy, spoiled people who didn't understand that a good wife doesn't mind working hard for her family.

Helen broiled steaks, hamburgers and chicken. She served salads made of iceberg lettuce and sliced tomatoes covered with bottled dressing and warmed up cans of peas and carrots. She didn't insist that her children finish everything on their plates and she threw out most of the leftovers despite her mother's disapproval.

While Leah scrounged for the cheapest cuts of meat, Golda demanded the most expensive. Her primary instruction to Rachel, the daughter-in-law who lived next door and shopped for her, was, "get me the good stuff," a phrase she repeated in English to make sure Rachel understood her.

When it came to food Golda knew exactly what she wanted – costly steaks, roast beef and other meats definitely not designed for an old lady who often couldn't be bothered to put in her teeth. To make it edible, she'd boil the meat until it was reduced to a soft mush guaranteed to make anyone else in the kitchen lose their appetite.

Cont.

It was clearly a waste of money however, as Rachel said, "What the old lady wants, the old lady gets. If it keeps her happy, it's worth the money. Otherwise she'll drive me crazy with all of her complaining and eventually my husband will get it for her anyway. "Heaven forbid his precious mama doesn't have everything she wants."

Golda believed that no meal was complete unless it included a good stiff drink. Conveniently, the few words Golda could pronounce properly in English included, "Southern Comfort." She generally finished about a quart of this 100 proof bourbon each week. If Rachel was slow getting her another bottle Golda just asked her grandson Kenny to buy it for her.

The owner of the nearby Parkway Liquors knew the family and didn't hesitate to give whiskey to a 12-year-old. "Here's some *schnopps* for grandma," he'd say, confident that Rachel would come in later to pay him.

When people were around, Golda sipped the Southern Comfort from a water glass. If she thought no one was watching, she drank straight from the bottle. If anyone suggested she slow down, Golda just smiled and said, "But you never saw me drunk."

It never occurred to anyone that they had probably never seen her completely sober.

When the street was quiet again, Golda turned to Leah. "So Mrs. Schwartz, this Lester, are you keeping company with him?"

"He's just someone at my school. He doesn't know the work as well as I do, so sometimes I stay after class and go over the lessons with him. The cafeteria is open late and we get tea and talk."

Leah attended night school at nearby Christopher Columbus High School, taking English for foreigners. Golda thought that was a waste of time. "I speak Yiddish perfectly well. Why bother with another language?" she had asked when Leah suggested that after 30 years in this country Golda might improve her English. "The people I want to talk to speak my language. Anyone else has something to say to me, they can learn Yiddish."

Cont.

While Golda had been a housewife her whole life and had always lived surrounded by her protective family, Leah had helped her husband run a candy store until he died. She was accustomed to being out in the world. Leah could speak, read and write English fairly well. This proficiency had earned her straight A's in the beginning English class, where the teacher told her she was his best student, a comment she repeated to everyone.

When that class was over, she re-enrolled and was surprised to find a different teacher in front of the class. She'd been promoted to the next grade. Now she was expected to learn geography, advanced math, history and other useless subjects.

Her teenaged granddaughter, Sarah, tried to help Leah with her homework, but it didn't work out.

"Who cares where Africa is?" Leah asked. "I'm not going there. Who would I know?"

"Let's try the math," said Sarah. "If you have half a pie and want to feed six people, how much pie does each person get?"

"That's ridiculous," said Leah. "Who serves half a pie to six people? I'd make another pie before they arrived. If they dropped in unexpectedly they could all eat stewed fruit instead. Remember, I told you, you should always make sure there's plenty of stewed fruit in the house. It's cheap and lasts a long time."

After a few weeks of failing grades, Leah marched into the director's office and demanded that she be put back into her old class. For the next several years she faithfully repeated the beginner's class, smiling smugly when the teachers praised her work, getting straight A's, always ready to help fellow students like Lester.

"I was thinking of inviting Lester to join me at the Senior Citizens Center some time," said Leah. "But I'm not sure. It hasn't been the same lately."

Leah was president of the Tea Committee at the Center, which meant she got the first chance to grab leftovers while she was cleaning up. She carried an extra-large purse on party days. If there was something particularly

Cont.

appetizing being served, she'd slip some of it into her bag before the party began, just in case there weren't any leftovers. Lately, she'd noticed people frowning at her when she filled her purse with goodies and she was afraid that her membership on the hospitality committee was almost over.

"Instead of taking this Lester to your crowded club, you should make another cake and bring it to him in his apartment," said Golda. "This time use more sugar, a little frosting isn't a bad idea. A man likes some sweetness from a woman."

"I know what a man likes from a woman," said Leah. "You don't have to tell me. I'm not going to go to the house of a man who lives alone. How would it look?"

"Who wants to look? Lester is our age? Getting close to 80? You're afraid he'll grab you by the hair and throw you on the bed? You should be so lucky."

"I don't like that kind of talk, Mrs. Rosen. I know from personal experience that men can't be trusted."

"Maybe you think he's lying, that he has a wife at home and wants someone on the side?" said Golda.

"Shame on you," said Leah. "He lost his wife in the camps and didn't remarry. He's a survivor." Leah touched the inside of her wrist indicating that Lester had a number tattooed there. "I don't know if he has any family here or if they were all lost. I don't want to ask questions about what he went through."

Golda was silent for a moment. "You're right, it's best not to pry about the past," she said. "But life goes on, no reason you two can't get together. Maybe you think he's after your money? All the pennies you save by buying food no one wants?"

"What do you know about the value of pennies, Mrs. Rosen?" said Leah. "You arrived in this country before the war and after your sons had established a good business. They gave you everything you wanted, you never had to do anything on your own. Whenever you want to go someplace, one of your sons drives you in his big, fancy car. No one thinks of asking you to take a bus or train or even to walk too far. If I want to go someplace Helen says, 'Don't worry about my

Cont.

mom, she can take care of herself.' And I can. I have to."

"You think you're the only one who's suffered?" said Golda. "You came over well before the Nazis arrived in Poland. Did you ever wonder why my sons came over without me? Young men were being forced into the Polish army.

They had to escape. I stayed behind to take care of my sick husband who couldn't travel." Golda stared straight ahead, not looking at Leah. "I was terrified. I didn't know what I would do if they closed the border. Yet I had to wait for my husband to die before I could leave."

Leah looked directly at Golda, not speaking until she finally turned and their eyes met. "But you did make it, Mrs. Rosen. And when you arrived everything was golden. Do you want to know why I came over so early?" Leah took a deep breath, raising her bosom.

"Remember, I don't come from a poor little peasant village like you. I was raised in Warsaw, a sophisticated, cultured city," she said, exhaling and deflating her bosom. "I was raised in a rich, educated and well-respected family. I was the oldest girl in my large family, I had to help with everything but I knew my future held a good match and a nice home of my own.

"Finally the matchmaker made the arrangements—she found a wealthy, handsome man for me. However, when he came to the house to meet me he got a look at my younger sister, a pretty, spoiled girl. Spoiled like you, Mrs. Rosen." Leah clenched her large hands into fists, realized what she had done and tried to relax them.

"He didn't care what agreement had been made. He decided that my little sister was the girl he wanted," she said. "And he got her."

"Those things happened, I know. You're lucky you were in a city. In a small village everyone knows everyone else's business."

"Even in a city the size of Warsaw, everyone knew. Wherever I went, I heard people talking about it. I was too embarrassed to think about having the matchmaker make another arrangement," said Leah.

Cont.

"My father sent me to America to avoid the shame. He got in touch with some relatives who arranged for me to marry Jake. You remember my Jake? He was a good man, a hard worker, but from a lower class," she said. "I arrived here just in time for the Depression. We slaved in our store to make ends meet. Believe me, Mrs. Rosen, no one paved the streets with gold for me.

"At first I got a few letters from home, however once the war started, nothing," she said. "I never saw any of them again."

"That's a hard story you tell Leah, but we all have stories," said Golda. "You must have heard that I didn't only have sons, that my oldest was a girl. Her name was Shoshanna, you know that's who our granddaughter Sarah is named after. Do you also know that my daughter was married well before the war started? That she had a baby, a little girl whose birthday would be today. My first grandchild. No one talks about that child anymore, no one celebrates her birthday. No one but me.

"When my boys said it was time to leave, my daughter's husband didn't believe them. He thought they were jealous that he had a successful business. He said Hitler would never reach Poland. I begged him to listen. He refused," Golda said. "He thought he was smarter than my boys. He and my daughter and my granddaughter stayed behind. They all died in the camps."

"You have to be grateful you got here, Leah," Golda said, suddenly realizing she was using the woman's given name. "You stayed alive, got married, had children and grandchildren who are alive. If not for the sister who took your fiancé you might have stayed in Warsaw and been killed with the rest of your family."

Leah sniffed and stared at Golda. "I'm not a fool," she said. "You don't have to tell me what happened in Europe. But if not for that girl I would have had an easy, rich life in Warsaw," she said. "So maybe we don't live forever. No one does. But while we were alive I'd live like a queen. No, Golda, I won't forgive that girl."

The two old women sat quietly on the bench, nothing left to say. They closed their eyes, lifted their chins, tried to catch the last rays of the sun on their wrinkled faces. However the sun was ready to set and

Cont.

a cool wind started to blow. It ruffled Golda's straight white hair and Leah's curly grey hair.

Golda checked that her bulky white cardigan was buttoned. Leah stretched her blue woolen jacket over her chest and zipped it up. After a few minutes, Golda turned to Leah.

"Maybe you're right, Leah, going to his house is too much," said Golda. "Still, if this Lester seems like a nice man maybe you should give him a chance. But be smart. Instead of making another cake, suggest he take you to a show. Make it clear he'll be paying, that you want to go in a taxi. See what happens. Play hard to get. No more free cakes."

Golda started to giggle. "If you need a chaperone I could come along," she said. "Just to make sure there's no funny business I'll have one of my boys give me a good, strong belt to carry in my purse."

Leah giggled too. "Just what I need," she said. "A drunken chaperone who'll probably forget her teeth. That'll keep him in his place."

"So, *machitanister*, how about coming inside and having some Southern Comfort?" said Golda. "It's getting chilly out here. A little *schnopps* will warm us up."

"Sounds like a good idea," said Leah. "And maybe a piece of your cake too."

On The Beach
by
S Berenstein

When he called, I answered my phone as fast as I could. On some level I knew it was dangerous, but I couldn't resist. After a few brief pleasantries he invited me to go for a run. I told him I felt rusty as a runner, but I'd meet him for a walk on the beach, instead. My daughter was four months old and I'd lost some of the baby weight, but I was still nursing and not doing strenuous exercise, yet. I didn't tell him any of that, of course. I just agreed to meet at our usual spot.

The uncanny part was that I'd dreamt about him two nights earlier. In the dream we were running and he said, like he used to, "You're a good runner. One foot in front of the other, that's all you have to do." I didn't tell him about my dream, either. Although I couldn't help wondering, did he ever dream about me?

Now, I had to wait three days until I saw him. Instantly, I regressed into a teenage girl. If the sun came out, it meant he still loved me. If the baby woke up, he didn't. I felt guilty and tried to stop, but how could I make the time roll by? When Esther did wake up, I took her out in the backyard. I put the umbrella up over her playpen and worked on my suntan — squeezing lemon juice on my hair to coax out the sunlight. Later, I started Paul's favorite dinner, but I was so preoccupied I scorched the rice. Then, I got another guilt attack. *Paul* was the one who was delighted when I asked, "Do we really need birth control?" It was time to stop daydreaming and be grateful for what I had.

Soon enough, Robert was walking towards me on the white sand with a huge smile on his face. His lopsided smile and the way he moved forward on those long legs with that characteristic loping

Cont.

stride hit me, suddenly, as if we were in a raft going over Niagara Falls and we'd been thrown overboard — we were immediately in the rushing water with each other. I took a deep breath and dug my toes in the sand to slow myself down. We put our arms around each other and he held me tight, lingering a little, before we both pulled away.

"How are you? I miss you!" he said.

"I'm good," I replied, wishing I felt free enough to say I missed him, too.

"You look just the same — tan, long sun-streaked hair and everything."

"You, too. But I think you've grown," I tilted my head up to catch his warm, brown eyes.

"Nah, you've just shrunk," he laughed. And his eyes lit up, crinkling around the edges. He threw himself down on the sand and patted the spot next to him, "What's new?"

I sat down. "So much has happened," I said, buying myself time, "I don't know where to begin."

"Last I knew you were dating that guy, Paul," he said, staring straight ahead at the ocean.

I couldn't think. It seemed like forever before I could find the words, "Yeah, now we live together." I watched him as he shut his eyes, briefly, and sighed.

"Lucky him," he muttered.

"Well, I don't know." I gave a little wave, trying to undo what he'd said. "And we have a baby girl, now. Esther," I added, wincing. Now, I was the one who closed my eyes. I wanted to add and I've been dreaming of *you*, but I succeeded in holding myself back.

"Oh," was all he said, but there was so much more in his voice than that simple word.

"So, you're happy?" He let out a strange, hard laugh. my stomach lurched. "Sure." Had he detected the fleeting pause before I answered? He probably had. He was silent and I could see the tension in his face.

Cont.

"I was worried that I couldn't make enough money before. Or that I would let you down, somehow. Uhm, I know it's probably too late." His voice trailed off. "It's my fault I wasn't ready. You had to think about your biological clock, duh. But now I *am* ready. I'm sorry. I shouldn't be blurting this out."

It felt like the air between us was throbbing. I didn't want to stop him, but I was afraid to

encourage him, too. We both stared silently at the glittering ocean.

"Look, Robert. It's so sunny that when the waves break it refracts the light." Refracts,

splinters, my mind was going everywhere.

He stared at me, silently asking his question about us, I assumed, but then he turned

towards the ocean, "You're always ecstatic when you're on the beach, aren't you?"

"I miss running here," I agreed. Softly, I added, "Those were some of the best times of

my life, running on the beach with you."

"I know. Me, too." He looked at me intently, got quickly to his feet and loped down to the edge of the water, then stooped to pick up a stone or a shell, turned and walked rapidly along the sand.

Tears came to my eyes as I watched him, but I brushed them away, roughly.

After a few minutes he walked back towards me, staying close to the waves hitting the shore. He gestured for me to join him.

I looked at him and the ocean. Both were full of unknown depths and beauty, in addition

to potential danger. And yet, I *kept* looking at him as I scrambled to my feet and walked forward,

Cont.

staring at the appealing, masculine shape of his body and his sandy, brown hair falling in his
eyes. I wanted to touch him, smell him, taste him — the familiarity of him felt so good. "I think we have some catching-up to do," I said rapidly. "Before I …" Whatever I was
starting to say dropped right out of my head when I noticed that his face was flushed. I knew
that was how he looked when he was trying not to cry.

    He rubbed his eyes with the back of his hand. "I've been working a lot and dating some women, here and there," he said, in an abrupt cadence.

    "Okay," I said, but I couldn't look at him.

    "I haven't found anyone, obviously."

    "Yeah," I looked up and held his eyes for a long minute. "I couldn't respond, before. You know how I feel about you, still feel. Even though I shouldn't, now. But, oh God. You and your timing!" Tears filled my eyes and I walked ahead of him as I looked out at the coastline. Then, I broke into a run. By the time I turned around to look at him, again, he was the size of a child in the distance. The song "Row, row, row your boat, gently down the stream. Merrily, merrily, merrily, merrily, life is but a dream," floated through my head. I laughed and ran into the ocean until I was in the water up to my waist. I splashed around and then, slowly, walked up towards the dry sand. I felt the water from my wet shorts dripping down my legs and the sand sticking to my feet as I waited for Robert to catch up with me.

    As he approached, he took off his jacket. "Even this time of year when the water is still pretty cold you don't let that stop you. Here, wear this," He wrapped the jacket around me.

    "Thanks." In fact, I felt flushed and not cold at all, but nothing could have persuaded me to reject what he was offering. "So," I said, "you've been thinking about kids?"

    "Well," he coughed into his fist, "Not kids in general. Kids with *you.*"

Cont.

There was no turning back, now. This was what we were talking about. I closed my eyes on and off as I listened to him. He told me that he knew he had blown it by not being ready before. But he was ready now, *more* than ready. He said he would love having a baby with me and he was confident that the two of us would hang in there. "I can imagine us laughing when we're sleep deprived, or about dirty diapers," he said, smiling at me. But his main point was that he believed we'd have a good chance of succeeding because of the strength of the love between us. The hardest thing would be taking me away from Paul, of course, and being the cause of complications and disruptions for baby Esther so, he'd understand if I couldn't do that. But if I did, he would try very hard to make it work. At the tail end of his 'speech,' he said, "I love the name Esther." But then he added, "I probably shouldn't have said that."

I would have laughed at that part, under ordinary circumstances, but instead we stared at each other for an undecipherable period of time.

"Please. Can we slow down? Let's walk," I said.

"Sure," he agreed, looking down at the sand.

I stepped back and let him move several yards ahead of me. Everything he'd said was spinning around and I felt as if I was about to faint. Was I angry at him for daring to make his proposal, even after I'd told him I had a baby with Paul? But maybe I'd subtly invited it. Certainly, in my heart I had longed for him to say it. And it felt good to know how he felt. How could I not feel tempted? Maybe he had guessed that would happen. I knew Robert well enough to know that once he made a commitment, he would hang in there. Then, I started thinking about a night we once spent in the Santa Cruz mountains,

Cont.

deep in the middle of the redwoods. We had both woken up before dawn and spontaneously decided to have breakfast in the woods. We'd filled a thermos with coffee, put bagels, cream cheese and fruit in a backpack, and hiked slowly up the hill, looking back to watch the sun rise on the horizon.

Robert and I had always shared a sense of awe, a magical feeling about nature. I imagined telling him what I was remembering. Although, I knew it was an invitation I wasn't ready to make. Still, it was tempting and my regret was palpable. I focused on a surfer paddling towards the waves and then catching one, riding it for a while and falling, but looking like he loved the act of catching it on the upside and crashing on the downside. It reminded me of another beautiful moment with Robert when we'd stayed at a small bed and breakfast, on the beach. We had slept together with the window open and heard the ocean waves as we slept. When we woke, we'd taken each other to the tip of orgasm and back again, over and over, like a sequence of small waves leading to a larger one and then the crash. My throat tightened and I fought back the desire to cry, it was so vivid. I couldn't stop myself. I ran to catch up with him, then.

He looked down at me, "You are such a pip squeak," he burst into laughter. "That first time we went running, you were so surprised that you could do it."

"Yeah, and I told myself I couldn't catch up with you because you were so much taller than me. Not because you were more athletic or because you're a man," I teased him, with a smile, but in an emphatic tone. I took his hand and pulled him back so we were walking at the same pace. But then I let go of his hand. I wasn't sure I wanted to tip the scale in his favor.

"You're the Champ," He grinned. "I've always liked calling you that, the same way my father called me, Champ."

Cont.

"I like it, too," I laughed, thinking of his consistently kind encouragement, "And I like pip squeak, too." He was the best boyfriend I ever had, I thought. Although, I did not say that out loud. Still, I was curious about the possibility, his "hope." And terrified, too. I stepped back and let him walk slightly ahead of me. How could I be sure he was ready? And what about Paul? It seemed more significant to me, now, that Paul and I had never gotten married. We had kept postponing it because it was hard to find a time when all of our friends and relatives could come to a wedding. Then I got pregnant. Did the fact that we never got married represent something about not being fully in love? An image came to my mind of Paul running his hands through his curly hair. Then, the shape of his handsome face as he turned to look at me. On the surface, these were small things, but what they truly meant to me was more than that. I loved his curly hair, the spring in his step, the sound of his laughter when I teased him about his "excellent bones." He was a good man and a solid man. How could I betray our family of three, even though we would still share custody of Esther? The words of Robert Frost came to mind, from "The Road Not Taken—Two roads diverged in a yellow wood," and something about thinking back with a sigh because of taking the less traveled road? Of course, I had no idea what Robert Frost meant or if I even had the words right, but it made me remember how time stopped with Robert, that I wanted to make passionate love with Robert. It was my questions about commitment or right and wrong that were tripping me up. But those things *were* important.

I looked up and noticed Robert standing there, trying to catch my eyes.

"When I first went running with you, I was out of shape," I said, trying to pick up where we left off, "You took me above and beyond those yoga classes and I got some noticeable calf and thigh muscles. You helped me build up my confidence, in a serious way." And not only with exercise, I thought. I never did explain to him my penchant for sexy, bad boys, I realized.

Cont.

Over and over, I had been seduced by those exciting beginnings, then betrayed by the selfishness or the cheating. Why hadn't I told him what a relief it was when I finally felt attracted to a sweetheart like him?

"Well, it was my pleasure."

His voice brought me out of my reverie and I smiled at him. Apart from my stint as a
cheerleader in high school — which had led briefly to popularity based on loud cheers, high kicks, an enthusiasm and flirtatiousness that relied on eye contact and what Danny, my high school boyfriend, had derisively and publicly called my 'seductive hair flipping technique'—sports had been an unexplored chapter in my life before Robert. And the difference between Danny, who had deliberately embarrassed me, and Robert? It didn't get any clearer than that.

Robert chortled, bringing me back to the present, again. He was standing on his toes. "I'm not only still running," he said, "but I'm growing. I'm one inch more than six feet, four," he laughed.

"Yeah, right," I laughed, too. "I have to start exercising, more. I have baby weight to lose."

"I can't tell," he said. "All you need to do is focus on feeling good and exercising every day. That'll do it."

"You're right." It was so typical of Robert to be kind in that way, even though I knew the extra pounds were noticeable. I looked at him, gratefully. "I'm glad you still believe that I'm capable as a runner. No one has done that for me before. And I always hear your voice, when I go running, saying, one foot in front of the other, that's *all* you have to do."

"You did the same for me, in other ways" he asserted, and I was hit, again, by a tender memory. In the beginning, Robert and I

Cont.

had had wild make-out sessions in the car or on the beach at night under a blanket. But then he would pull away, saying he had a call to make or an early meeting. Finally, he told me what had happened with his ex-wife, Lisa. She had mocked him when he couldn't get hard. Humiliated him, badly. He'd been relieved when I was patient and loving and confident that it would work out between us. And it *had* worked out. It had more than worked out. We had a genuine chemistry. And we were gentle with each other about our insecurities. It had been reciprocal and smooth between us.

Yet the most important thing of all, having a baby, had been anything but. I'd assumed, given how much we agreed, generally, that we'd feel the same way about having children. It had been such a blow.

Robert looked at me briefly and then walked on ahead. A flash of sun in my eyes brought an image of Paul bent over the changing table, catching and kissing Esther's toes as she squealed at her father's tickle. Why wasn't that enough? I was hit by another wave of confusion. I walked along faster to catch up with Robert. When he turned and waited for me, I started to skip.

"You still skip like a little girl." He laughed in that boisterous way he had. "You used to do that to hide the fact that you were tired of running."

"I wasn't tired of running," I said, sounding defensive even to myself. "I like to skip."

"I know you do," he said, with a tender look in his eyes.

"I just remembered a dream I had, last night." As I started saying it, I knew it was flirtatious, but I went ahead. "It was an image of a spring where the water was rushing forward and spurting up freely out of the ground."

"Spurting?" Robert laughed, glancing at me with a suggestive look.

I laughed, too, but then I stopped and looked away. "It was about having access to creativity in relationships," I said quickly, but I didn't wait for his response. I started running ahead of him, and as

Cont.

I did, tears came to my eyes; Why did I say that? What about *Paul*? Robert caught up with me. "You're crying," he said. His voice was gentle.

"I know. I'm so confused." I wiped my eyes and looked up at him. "Let's keep walking, okay?"

"Sure," he said and he walked along slowly, careful not to look at me.

I walked behind him, taking deep breaths and gradually catching up with him.

He looked at me with his eyebrows raised, and reached for my hand, "Do you want to talk?"

"Not yet."

As we walked along together, I stumbled. He gripped my hand and I leaned into his firm grasp to steady myself.

"All of this is blinding and scary." I paused for a few beats. "*And* tempting. I just don't know," I said, careful not to look into his eyes.

"I understand. But I meant everything I said. Of course, you can't respond right away. I'll wait and let you take the lead."

"All right." I cleared my throat to hide the fact that I was choked up. It was a relief to feel the late afternoon breeze, then.

He bent down and I closed my eyes, wondering if he would put his lips to mine. But if he thought about doing that I would never know. It was my forehead he kissed. How would he interpret the sound I made then Gratitude? Sadness? Joy? It was all of those things.

As we walked across the beach together, on our way to the parking lot, Robert was swinging his hands. They looked twice their normal size as the evening shadows lengthened across the sand. We were silent during those last few minutes, turning back and looking wistfully at the waves. As we got to his car, we lingered before saying goodbye with a long look and then, a wave.

I stood there for that last minute, watching him pull away. As I walked towards my car I started hiccupping, I was trying so hard to hold back my tears. I couldn't bear to feel what was at stake and how much I loved him. Yet, I knew I had to go home, now. I loved Paul, too, although it was different. And I felt so lucky to have baby Esther. One foot in front of the other. That's all I have to do, I thought. But the parking lot looked empty, now that he was gone.

Contributors

Jane Risdon is the co-author of 'Only One Woman,' with Christina Jones (Headline Accent) and 'Undercover: Crime Shorts,' (Plaisted Publishing), as well as having many short stories published in numerous anthologies. She has written for several online and print magazines such as Writing Magazine, Electric Press, and The Writers' and Readers' Magazine. She is a regular guest on international internet podcasts including UK Crime Book Club (UKCBC), Donnas Interviews Reviews and Giveaways, and on radio shows such as theauthorsshow .com,, and The Brian Hammer Jackson Radio Show. Undercover: Crime Shorts is being used by Western Kentucky University, Kt.USA, in an Introduction to Literature Class, for second year students from Autumn 2021. Before turning her hand to writing Jane worked in the International Music Business, alongside her musician husband, working with musicians, singer/songwriters, and record producers. They also facilitated the placement of music in movies and television series. Earlier in her career she also worked for the British Ministry of Defence in Germany, the Foreign and Commonwealth Office, London. https://janerisdon.com
Jane is represented by Linda Langton of Langton's International Literary
Agency in New York City, New York USA.

Rekha Valliappan is an award-winning multi genre writer of short stories, poetry and creative nonfiction. Her credits include Litro Magazine, The Cabinet of Heed, The Saturday Evening Post (fiction); Ann Arbor Review, The Pangolin Review, Nixes Mate Review (poetry); The Museum of Americana: A Literary Review, The Blue Nib, Adelaide Literary Magazine (creative nonfiction); Bending Genres, Critical Reads, Dawntreader (flash fiction); and various other places. Her writing has earned nominations for the Pushcart Prize and Best of the Net.

Roger Knight. Having become a reluctant retiree, I have embarked upon a replacement career of writing, now that I become stuck in those valleys of reflection. To date I have published one Collection of poems, Poems of Passage and have had several poems and short stories published in various anthologies.

****

Elisha Alladina is a social worker, published poet, expressive artist, and singer/songwriter from Canada. She has had 15 poems, a creative nonfiction piece, and a children's short story published to date for various zines, anthologies, and online publications, as well as a poetry chapbook, Internal Eyes(2022). Her song/poem Christmas Candles was nominated for Publication Of The Month on spillwords.com, and is available on all streaming platforms along with several of her other songs. In 2007, she made the Top 125 on Canadian Idol.

****

J A Newman has published five books: NO ONE COMES CLOSE a memoir, BAY OF SECRETS a family mystery and two rom-coms: WHERE THERE'S A WILL and the sequel LOSING THE WILL. Her latest work is her anthology THE OTHER SIDE OF LIFE. She has written many articles for This England and Evergreen magazines and The Writers and Readers' magazine. She has also had historical short stories published in two anthologies for the Caradon Hill Heritage Project and one for the charity Help4Heroes. She was born and raised in Bexley, Kent and enjoyed a hairdressing career in various locations before retiring to South East Cornwall where she found her writing voice. She is currently living in West Norfolk with her husband. Her blog: julieannnewman.wordpress.com and Facebook @J.A.Newman.author

LaVern Spencer McCarthy, has written and published nine books, five of poetry and five of fiction. Her work has appeared in Writers and Readers Magazine, Meadowlark Reader, Agape Review, Fenechty Publications, Metastellar. Down In The Dirt, Mouthfeel, Fresh Words Magazine. Wicked Shadows Press, Midnight Magazine. and others. She resides in Blair Oklahoma where she is currently writing her sixth book of short stories.

****

Heather Haigh
Heather is a sight-impaired spoonie and emerging working-class writer from Yorkshire. When not scribbling words, she enjoys waving a camera around or clacking knitting needles.

****

Hannah McIntyre currently resides in Edinburgh whilst she undertakes her Creative Writing Masters degree. Previously, she lived and studied at Lancaster University where she began her training as a writer. She has published short stories in both Emerging Worlds and From Arthur's Seat as she works on completing her first novel

Julie Watson is an Isle of Wight writer and the author of two collections of personal travel stories. Her most recent book is [Travel Takeaways: Around the World in Forty Tales](), published by Beachy Books in April 2023.

****

Meredith Stephens is a recently retired professor from South Australia. Her work has appeared in *Transnational Literature, The Blue Mountain Review, Agape Review, Borderless, The Font - A Literary Journal for Language Teachers, The Writers' and Readers' Magazine, The Journal of Literature in Language Teaching, Reading in a Foreign Language,* and anthologies published by Demeter Press, Canada. She spends her retirement gathering material for new stories as she sails in Australian waters and beyond.

****

Con Chapman is a Boston-area writer, author of "Rabbit's Blues: The Life and Music of Johnny Hodges" (Oxford University Press), winner of the 2019 Book of the Year Award by Hot Club de France; "Kansas City Jazz: A Little Evil Will Do You Good" (Equinox Publishing); and "Don Byas: Sax Expatriate," forthcoming in 2024 from University Press of Mississippi.

His work has appeared in The Atlantic, The Boston Globe, The Boston Herald, and a number of literary magazines.

Barbara Hull. Barbara Hull, a Mancunian by birth, is a writer, linguist and professional translator. She now lives in North Yorkshire

****

Michael Shawyer. Despite early signs of penmanship Mick's journey through life showed little sign of story-telling and it wasn't until 2018, (fishing for yellow fin tuna in South Africa), that he started punching the keys on his laptop. He hit some mid-table success with competitions and magazines publishing his work. Lit eZine Magazine, Ariel Chart, Secret Attic, Neurological Magazine, Apricot Press, Shorts Magazine, Revolutionary Press, Fictionette Magazine, A Thousand Lives & More Magazine.
In December 2021 he moved to a Township in Kwa Zulu Natal. The only white person in a self-governing Zulu community. He is currently homeless in the UK.

***8

Linda Hibbin is a septuagenarian and a mosaic artist living near the Essex coast in the U.K. Linda began writing during the Pandemic. She joined online creative writing courses organized by the Workers' Educational Association. Writing quirky fiction is her first love. These narratives often reflect comical self-observation inspired by her life experiences and the people and situations around her. Since 2020, Linda's work has been published internationally. Publishers include *Dreich Mag, Potato Soup Journal, Reedsy, and Visual Verse. Writefluence* has printed her short stories in nine anthologies. Linda recently won 1st prizes in the *Pen to Print Short Story Competition* and the *Worcester LitFest Flash Fiction Competition*

Books in USA: "Escape" (2019 - Royal Hawaiian Press), "Anomaly" (2020 - Royal Hawaiian Press) Books in Spain:"La fuga" (2019 - Royal Hawaiian Press), "Anomalia" (2019 - Royal Hawaiian Press) Books in Germany: "Die Anomalie" (2020 - Der Romankiosk)
Books in Canada: "The Prisoner Of Infinity" (2022 - Ukiyoto Publishing), "And On Earth without Changes" (2022 - Ukiyoto Publishing), "The Worries Of A Not So Dead Man" (2022 - Ukiyoto Publishing)Books in Poland: "Deathbirth" (2008 - Armoryka publishing house), "Anima vilis" (2010 - Initium publishing house), "Grobbing" (2012 - Novae Res publishing house), "Deathbirth and other stories" (2012 & 2017 - Agharta & Armoryka publishing house), "Z życia Dr Abble" (2013 - Agharta publishing house), "Anomalia" (2016 - Forma publishing house), "Ucieczka" (2017 - Dom Horroru publishing house), "Nie w inność" (2019 - Waspos publishing house) & "Nieznośna niewyraźność bytu" (2022 - Saga Egmont), "Obyś żył w ciekawych czasach" (2023 - Św. Wojciecha)

****

DC Diamondopolous is an award-winning short story, and flash fiction writer with stories published internationally in print and online magazines, literary journals, and anthologies. DC's stories have appeared in: *Sunlight Press, Progenitor, 34th Parallel, So It Goes: The Literary Journal of the Kurt Vonnegut Museum and Library, Lunch Ticket,* and others. DC has been nominated twice for both the Pushcart Prize and Best of the Net Anthology. She lives on the California central coast with her wife and animals.
dcdiamondopolous.com

Andrew Senior is a writer of short literary and speculative fiction, based in Sheffield, UK. He lives with his wife and offspring and writes whenever he can find the time to do so. He prefers it to talking. His work has recently appeared, or is forthcoming, in various publications, including Isele Magazine, Postbox Magazine, Litro Magazine and the Honest Ulsterman. Visit andrewseniorwriting.weebly.com

****

Chiara Vascotto is a writer with a keen interest in dance. Her work spans creative non-fiction, playwriting, and fiction. She has been published in Litro, Amaranth Magazine, and in The Dillidoun Review. Her short story Kadamati has recently won the writing competition A Blind Play of Social Forces. Chiara is thrilled to have performed in works by Michael Clark, Akram Khan and Boris Charmatz as a non-professional dancer. When not writing, Chiara works in consumer insights and branding. She comes from Trieste, Italy, and lives in London.

****

Andy Stuart is a retired family doctor. He and his wife have a small vineyard in South East Cornwall. In the past he has written satirical articles aimed at a medical readership under the guises of Dr Basil Bile and Dr Hugh Joverdraft. Over the last few years, he has had short stories published in Gin City 2, Write Time Anthology 2, Scribble Magazine, Flash Flood Journal, the Farnham Flash Festival Competition Winners Book, and the Tothill Tales and Tittle-Tattle anthology. He enjoys writing in the genres of cosy crime and situational humour, and also Flash Fiction. He is a founder member of the Tothill Scribblers, a group of aspiring writers who meet weekly to critique each other's literary outpourings. He has just completed writing an anthology of short stories with a medical flavour entitled 'All The Infections That The Sun Sucks Up'.

Jean Ende is a native NYer who is trying to exorcise her background by writing fiction largely based on her immigrant Jewish family. Her stories have been published in print and online magazines and anthologies in the US and England and recognized by major literary competitions. She is a former newspaper reporter, political publicist, corporate marketing executive and college professor. Her work can be seen at jeanendeauthor.com. Jean just finished writing her first novel and is looking for a publisher or agent.

****

S. Berenstein, is a fiction writer for half of the week and a psychologist for the other half. Her work has been published in Litbreak, Drip Lit, Literary Yard, Hot Flash, The California Council of the Arts Journal and more. Her flash fiction was listed under 'Notable Stories' in Brilliant Flash Fiction.

****

Publishing Guide

All Your Stories (Magazine)
https://allyourstories.com
United Kingdom
We accept short stories, essays, fiction and non-fiction, travel tales, articles on lifestyle and much more check our contribution guide for word counts and subjects if you have accompanying sketches or pictures, please attach them as jpg. files.
All pages need to be numbered and show name and email address in Ms Word not PDF.
A short bio and picture should be attached to your submission.
No payment currently.
We do not accept anything sexually explicit.
If your submission is accepted for publication, you will receive a free online copy of the magazine.
We do not claim copyright this remains with the author.
This is a new magazine to give new and experienced writers an opportunity to be published.
Disclaimer:
The views expressed in published contributions in this magazine are those of the individual author and do not necessarily reflect those of All Your Stories Magazine or its Staff.
editor@allyourstories.com
submissions@allyourstories.com
(C) All Your Stories 2024 All rights reserved

Printed in Great Britain
by Amazon